Praise for

Death by Sudoku

"The start of a great new amateur-sleuth series . . . Kaye Morgan is a talented storyteller who will go far in the mystery genre."   —*The Best Reviews*

"The characters are likable . . . Sudoku plays an integral role, and puzzles are presented in various places for the reader to solve."   —*Gumshoe Review*

"Will have readers sharpening their pencils and their wits as they tackle this complicated mystery . . . Edgy and amusing."   —*Romantic Times*

Sinister Sudoku

Kaye Morgan

BERKLEY PRIME CRIME, NEW YORK

THE BERKLEY PUBLISHING GROUP
Published by the Penguin Group
Penguin Group (USA) Inc.
375 Hudson Street, New York, New York 10014, USA
Penguin Group (Canada), 90 Eglinton Avenue East, Suite 700, Toronto, Ontario M4P 2Y3, Canada
(a division of Pearson Penguin Canada Inc.)
Penguin Books Ltd., 80 Strand, London WC2R 0RL, England
Penguin Group Ireland, 25 St. Stephen's Green, Dublin 2, Ireland (a division of Penguin Books Ltd.)
Penguin Group (Australia), 250 Camberwell Road, Camberwell, Victoria 3124, Australia
(a division of Pearson Australia Group Pty. Ltd.)
Penguin Books India Pvt. Ltd., 11 Community Centre, Panchsheel Park, New Delhi—110 017, India
Penguin Group (NZ), 67 Apollo Drive, Rosedale, North Shore 0632, New Zealand
(a division of Pearson New Zealand Ltd.)
Penguin Books (South Africa) (Pty.) Ltd., 24 Sturdee Avenue, Rosebank, Johannesburg 2196,
South Africa

Penguin Books Ltd., Registered Offices: 80 Strand, London WC2R 0RL, England

This is a work of fiction. Names, characters, places, and incidents either are the product of the author's imagination or are used fictitiously, and any resemblance to actual persons, living or dead, business establishments, events, or locales is entirely coincidental. The publisher does not have any control over and does not assume any responsibility for author or third-party websites or their content.

SINISTER SUDOKU

A Berkley Prime Crime Book / published by arrangement with the author

PRINTING HISTORY
Berkley Prime Crime mass-market edition / August 2008

Copyright © 2008 by The Berkley Publishing Group.
Sudoku puzzles and *Composition in Blue, Red, and Green* by Kaye Morgan.
Cover art and logo by Trisha Krauss.
Cover design by Annette Fiore.
Interior text design by Laura K. Corless.

ISBN: 978-0-425-22306-2

BERKLEY® PRIME CRIME
Berkley Prime Crime Books are published by The Berkley Publishing Group,
a division of Penguin Group (USA) Inc.,
375 Hudson Street, New York, New York 10014.
The name BERKLEY PRIME CRIME and the BERKLEY PRIME CRIME design
are trademarks belonging to Penguin Group (USA) Inc.

PRINTED IN THE UNITED STATES OF AMERICA

10 9 8 7 6 5 4 3 2 1

This one is for my family, who may occasionally find it disconcerting to have a writer in their midst, but they love me anyway.

And thanks as always to Michelle Vega, who suggested the green Mondrian. For all you Mondrian lovers out there, yes, I made up the painting.

Composition in Blue, Red, and Green: The Stolen Mondrian

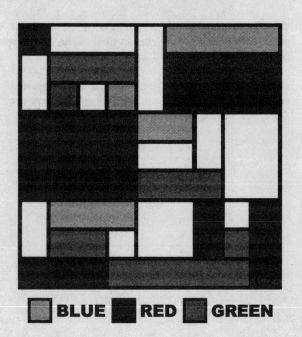

BLUE ■ RED ■ GREEN

PART ONE:
Naked Singles

It's a sexy name for one of the simplest, most intuitive techniques in the sudoku solver's arsenal. All it entails is looking for a space where clues in the intersecting row and column (and the surrounding nine-space subgrid) eliminate all but one candidate. A trained eye can spot a naked single even in a fairly sparse puzzle.

Oh, it's a fairly humble technique compared to the higher-order methods that slash complicated chains of logic across a puzzle and require props like bingo chips or colored pencils. For some people, familiarity breeds contempt. But I always get a feeling of satisfaction whenever the naked single opens up the first space on a puzzle. As someone once said, without a little bit of familiarity, you can't breed anything.

—Excerpt from *Sudo-cues* by Liza K

1

Liza Kelly opened the classroom door, her particular hall of learning, if a bit spartan—a large desk up front, smaller desks bolted to the floor. In spite of its recent construction, the room seemed to suffer from indifferent maintenance, the off-white paint still fresh but already getting dingy, the floor scuffed. Liza took a deep breath of slightly stale air as she stepped inside. *A typical institutional space,* she thought, *except I never expected to be in this kind of institution.*

Beyond the heavily grated window she could see a high wall topped with razor wire. This was the minimum-security section of the Seacoast Correctional Facility, but it was a prison just the same.

Kevin Shepard entered the classroom behind her, pulling out a water bottle from his pocket and taking a sip. "Last class, huh?" he said, sounding relieved.

"You didn't have to come along every time," she told him.

"Maybe Ava and Michelle think it's a good idea for you to teach sudoku in the joint," Kevin growled. "I don't."

Liza's sudoku column had proven its popularity locally in the *Oregon Daily*. In fact, other papers around the region had picked it up, partly because Liza had gotten involved in several widely covered murder cases. Now larger markets across the country had expressed interest in the column written by her alter ego, Liza K.

Ava Barnes, Liza's childhood friend and managing editor of the *Oregon Daily*, couldn't be happier about the free advertising for her syndication efforts. But Michelle Markson, Liza's partner for several years in the trenches of Hollywood publicity, wanted more.

Her latest PR brainstorm had landed Liza in the grim confines of Seacoast Correctional, teaching inmates to sublimate their felonious impulses through sudoku. She thought she could detect Michelle's fine hand in the choice of high-profile prisoners as her students, but it could be the corrections department playing safe, or even a reflection of her own semicelebrity status. In any case, she didn't really see the need for Kevin to act as her bodyguard and said so.

"You know what Sheriff Clements calls this part of the prison?" she asked. "The penal extension."

Liza said that just as Kevin took another sip of water. He choked, and she looked at him closely. "Did that just come out your nose?"

"Nurgle." His denial came out more as a snort than a word.

Kevin coughed, took a deep breath, and chose a more diplomatic answer. "No comment."

"I'll take that as a yes, then." Liza looked toward the door. "Brace yourself. Here comes murderers' row."

Actually, Liza felt a little bad about teasing Kevin. She'd come up to her hometown of Maiden's Bay trying to clear her mind—her Hollywood career had estranged her from her husband and left her disillusioned with the celebrity rat race. Finding her old high school beau had been a pleasant surprise, and his more than warm welcome had been nicer still.

Then her husband, Michael, had turned up in town, hoping for reconciliation, and Liza found herself part of a very complicated triangle. It had started off isosceles, with Liza and Kevin pretty close and Michael at a distance. Finding out the seamy side of Kevin's job running a high-scale rustic inn had skewed the triangle again, with Michael coming closer and Kevin off on a point on his own.

In fact, until Michael had returned to La-la Land on a film script job, he and Liza had been awfully close. But Kevin had been trying to make up lost ground, taking her out to dinner—and appointing himself her bodyguard here.

The first inmate entered giggling. Ritz Tarleton was a short-timer, in for ten days on a DUI and disorderly conduct charge. Portland had proven much less tolerant of all-night partying and high-speed chases than L.A. Ritz owed her name and her money to her daddy's travel empire, Tarleton Tours. Liza wasn't sure where the girl's looks came from. Ritz wore her hair shaggy, dyed an improbable shade of red with a good inch of dirty blond roots showing along a ragged part. Liza knew this was The Look, but the combination with pretty but sharp features made Ritz resemble a fox—a rather vacuous, self-satisfied fox. Her forehead looked as if it had never suffered a wrinkle from worry or even thought. Liza wasn't sure whether that was due to money, celebrity, or Botox.

The next member of murderers' row was a cherubic-faced chubby guy a little younger than Liza and Kevin. Usually Cornelius (Conn) Lezat's Cupid's-bow lips seemed set in a pout about three seconds away from tears. In the days of his boy-genius glory, those overdone lips had usually been set in a cocky grin. Back then he seemed on the verge of forming a hardware and software empire to challenge Microsoft. Instead, he'd created a financial black hole to rival Enron—and got dubbed "the Scumsucker Lezat" by furious people all over the Northwest who'd lost investments and pensions in the debacle.

An even heavier man followed Conn, short and squat—the only real murderer in the group. In his earlier and leaner days, Fat Frankie Basso had gotten his hands pretty dirty. These days he called the shots for a good-sized criminal enterprise, trying to pitch that can-do American spirit against several Russian mobs operating in Portland. Basso nodded to Liza and Kevin, flashing them both a genial fatman's smile—one that never reached a pair of eyes that looked like chips of obsidian set under big, heavy brows. His thinning gray hair was brushed straight back. And although his jawline had softened along with his bulging belly, those cold eyes staring out over an eagle nose showed his former hardness—a murderous hardness that lived on within.

All of a sudden, Liza found herself glad that Kevin was around.

Fat Frankie wasn't in the joint for murder, though. He was serving the tail end of a two-year stretch for criminal conspiracy. The last member of the class was the veteran convict. Chris Dalen had spent more than a decade as a guest of the state. He had a lean, compact physique, a dancer's build—or a cat burglar's. That fit in with Dalen's claim to fame, breaking into a small museum to steal a pricey painting. Although it had been created almost ninety years ago by Piet Mondrian, the canvas rated as a masterpiece of modern art and was worth several million dollars. Dalen's refusal to reveal the location of the stolen artwork had kept him in a cell five times longer than Basso.

The years showed as Dalen stepped into the sunlight from the window. His skin had grown slack, the muscles stringy. The gray hair wasn't a surprise, but the matching complexion was. That wasn't just prison pallor, though. Dalen had suffered two heart attacks in the last six months. Liz wasn't sure whether that came from prison food or years of stress catching up with him. His condition had won him a release, though Liza had to wonder how much time the art thief had left to enjoy his freedom.

"So this is the big day, isn't it Chris?" she asked.

"Ze guards haff gotten ze orders," he said in a parody of a World War II bad-guy's accent. "After this class, we do der paperwork, und then I blow zis pop stand."

"Well, congratulations, Herr Dalen." Liza looked around as her students settled themselves into their seats. "Thank you all for taking part in these pilot sessions." Ritz responded with her patented giggle, Conn looked almost bashful, Fat Frankie gave a quick nod, and Chris Dalen gave her a grin that momentarily lit up his fine features.

"I'm really interested in seeing how you handled your last assignment," Liza went on.

Over the last ten days, they had talked a lot about sudoku puzzles. The basics seemed simple enough. Take a nine-by-nine grid and fill in the one possible solution based on the twenty-something number of clues given. All you have to do is use each of the numbers one through nine to fill in the nine spaces in each of the nine rows and columns. The grid is also broken into nine three-by-three subgrids whose nine spaces also must contain the magic digits one through nine.

Although sudoku depends on numbers, the puzzles require no arithmetical expertise—no addition, subtraction, or square roots needed. The solution depends on logic— eliminating possibilities for a given space and discovering the one and only possible inhabitant.

That wasn't to say that sudoku were easy. Consider a chessboard, an eight-by-eight grid with thirty-two squares occupied—and the multiplicity of permutations that can be worked across it.

Achieving a sudoku solution didn't require movement. Instead, a solver used a series of techniques that rose in complexity. In her newspaper column and in this class, Liza concentrated on what she called the twelve steps to sudoku perfection. Actually, there were only eleven techniques—the last involved peeking in the back of the book or magazine for the printed solution.

Some of the techniques were simple enough that even Ritz had mastered them. Others required time and practice—creating an educated eye to recognize certain sudoku situations. Still others played with probabilities in a way that came perilously close to the great sudoku taboo—guessing an answer.

And there were even more esoteric techniques out there, Liza knew. These were based on the kinds of complicated equations that most people encountered only on the blackboards in the background of that TV show where the math genius helped the FBI.

In her final assignment for the class, Liza had turned the tables. Instead of looking for a solution, the students had gotten the job of creating a problem. Liza gave them the world's most basic sudoku solution, a pretty obvious setup:

1	2	3	4	5	6	7	8	9
4	5	6	7	8	9	1	2	3
7	8	9	1	2	3	4	5	6
2	3	4	5	6	7	8	9	1
5	6	7	8	9	1	2	3	4
8	9	1	2	3	4	5	6	7
3	4	5	6	7	8	9	1	2
6	7	8	9	1	2	3	4	5
9	1	2	3	4	5	6	7	8

The class members also received a brief set of instructions and the challenge of figuring out how to remove answers from matching spaces to create a thirty-clue sudoku.

"Who'd like to start?" she asked.

That cut off the giggling from Ritz. Her elaborate attempts to avoid meeting Liza's eyes came straight out of junior high. Liza wanted to laugh, until she realized that Conn Lezat was doing the same thing.

Liza sighed. "I realize there was a good chance some of you couldn't see this project all the way through."

"Oh, that's all right, then." Ritz Tarleton's voice had regained that giggly tone.

"How far did you get?" Liza asked.

"Not very," Ritz admitted. "It was really hard!" She handed Liza an obviously incomplete grid. Liza felt her brows coming together as she looked it over.

"You filled all the spaces in the upper left and lower right boxes in numerical order. That used up more than half of your available clues—no wonder you had such a tough time trying to lay out the rest of the puzzle." Liza reached for her copy of the instruction packet that had accompanied the grids.

"There's no rule against it," Ritz piped up.

"Maybe not, but why would you do that?" Kevin had to ask.

As Ritz looked at him, her foxy face went from vacuous to predatory—the cunning little vixen scooping out a plump fowl. "I have a rep to maintain, for being . . . cutting edge."

Ritz licked her lips.

Liza did her best to keep her face calm, even as her hand clenched into fists. No doubt the warden and the prison administration would get annoyed if she smacked one of their charges. She decided to change the subject by turning to another class member. "How about you, Conn?"

Lezat had donned a pair of wire-frame eyeglasses, which he now pushed up on the abbreviated bridge of his nose. "I started out, then I came across a reference to this technique called Bowman's Bingo." He brought out a little envelope and poured out a little pile of those clear plastic disks some people used to mark bingo cards. Liza wondered how in hell Lezat had gotten his hands on those.

"This is a semi-recursive elimination technique that can be employed manually," the business whiz began. "I've got nine sets of these chips, each marked one through nine. Now, by picking a starting point, I put a possible number facedown . . ."

As he droned on, Liza shook her head. According to the online sudoku discussion sites, Bowman's Bingo embodied the logic both in the Forcing Chains and Nishio techniques. Some members even suggested that being able to do such a technique by hand spelled the end of sudoku solving.

She interrupted before Conn got into full lecture mode. "I'm aware of how it works," Liza said. "I'm also aware that this is an extremely advanced solving technique, while you were supposed to be creating a simple puzzle. How far did you get?"

"Well, ah . . ." Conn finally handed over a couple of pages of cryptic calculations and a grid with only three spaces filled in. Liza had to wonder if this was why Lezat's company had gone belly-up. Had he distracted himself with fancy ideas, plans, and strategies when he should have been taking care of business?

She turned to Fat Frankie, who gave her an almost genuine smile. The expression stayed on his face as he turned to his more hapless classmates—except he didn't bother to hide the contempt in his eyes. "It took a while, but I think I got this to work. I had a couple of guys check it out, and they all got the same answers."

1		3		5		7		9
	5		7		9		2	
					4			
	3		5		7		9	
5								4
	9		2		4		6	
		5				9		
	7		9		2		4	
9		2		4		6		8

He gave her five copies of the puzzle, plus a solution sheet.

Liza nodded, glancing over the puzzle. One thing she'd discovered—when Fat Frankie put his mind to something, he did a workmanlike job.

"That leaves you, Chris," Liza said, turning to her final student—her best, she also suspected. Chris Dalen didn't show it much, but he had a playful streak and a mind as agile as his body once had been. He handed her a sheet, and Liza felt a stab of disappointment. It looked as if he'd managed to put down even fewer clues than Ritz.

Dalen grinned at her expression—and passed over four more copies and the solution. "Zey tell us zat less is more," he said. "Und zo I got by witout all zat many clues." Liza did a quick count. Then she went back and did a slower one.

8								
9		5						
			2		6			
			5					
	6						8	
			1				7	9
	3				2			
			8		7			
			9		1			

"There are only seventeen clues here." She didn't even attempt to keep the amazement out of her voice. "That's the lowest number of clues that anyone has used to make a valid puzzle so far."

2

"How did you—" Liza began.

Chris Dalen simply waggled his eyebrows, replying, "Ve haff vays . . ."

Holding this gem of a puzzle, Liza felt mightily tempted to grab a pencil and begin checking it out. A glance over at Frankie Basso knocked that idea out of her head, however. Fat Frankie looked definitely put out over being upstaged, and it probably wasn't a good idea to tick off a Mafia Don, or shot-caller, or whatever organized crime rank that Basso held.

Liza frowned. If she as a civilian felt that, surely Chris, with his years in the joint, knew that fact far better. *Maybe it's because he's getting out today,* she thought. Then she thought, *Maybe it's a good thing he's getting out when he is.*

That wasn't the reason why she used Basso's sudoku for the class discussion, though. The assignment she had given was creating a puzzle with thirty clues—and Fat Frankie was the only class member who'd done that. The thunder-clouds gradually left the mobster's face as he started talking about his trials and triumphs constructing the sudoku.

"You said that as I took numbers away from the grid you gave me, I had to balance them out—"

"Mirror them," Liza said.

"Yeah, mirror. So I figured the easiest way was to make the bottom half of the puzzle match the top. That made it easy enough—pick out a number up top, then go for its reverse down below." He shook his head, frowning. "But then going back to figure out the whole puzzle again, that was a pain in the ass. Especially since that most basic sudoku you gave us made it so easy to cheat."

"I found that, too," Conn Lezat put in. "That's why I thought that maybe some sort of randomizing system . . ."

Liza let him drone on for a little more, thinking, *Sure, right, take a simple job and make it ridiculously more difficult.*

On the other hand, this was her first shot at teaching a class. If the students felt that the grid she'd handed out didn't work, Liza should at least consider what they had to say.

"Okay," she said, "I'll work up a less distracting grid in the future."

"That will keep the rechecking a bit more interesting," Chris Dalen said dropping his phony accent. "I bet this would have been a lot easier with one of those computer programs that keeps a running list of all the possible candidates for each space. Me, I wouldn't know." The art thief shrugged. "They won't let me anywhere near one."

"I thought they had computers here," Liza said.

"But not everyone has access," Fat Frankie explained. "F'rinstance, they think I might communicate with various associates." His smile was bland, as if that never happened.

"I use one every day," Ritz piped up. "After all, I have to update my blog."

The mobster gave her an *I rest my case* look.

Chris Dalen shrugged. "And even though I'm getting out today, there's still an order barring—What did they call it?—'unauthorized contacts' or something like that." He smiled at Liza's puzzled expression. "I guess they're afraid I was going to put the Mondrian up for auction on eBay."

Liza didn't know what to say to that, so she went back to discussing the techniques and choices Fat Frankie had made in constructing his sudoku.

When Liza finished, Ritz gave her head a sage shake. "Just as I thought," she said. "This is really, really hard." That predatory look came over her fox-face as she glanced over at Kevin again. "Ya know what I mean?" A little pink tongue tip appeared between the celebutante's lips.

Liza had to restrain herself from whacking the girl over the head. *With my luck, her teeth would click together, she'd bite off the end of her tongue, and I'd face a long court case over cruelty to prisoners. Not the best publicity for Liza K's syndicated sudoku column.*

Kevin only rolled his eyes.

The class finally came to an end, and Liza thanked her erstwhile students. "You were very good sports, taking part in this pilot program," she said.

"It's not as if we had to fit you into our busy schedules," Conn Lezat told her.

"When they asked me, I thought, 'What the hell?'" Fat Frankie admitted. "But—well, I came up with that damned puzzle, didn't I?"

"Better being in here than looking at walls and bars." Ritz shot another glance at Kevin as she spoke.

Chris Dalen had to smile at the girl's honesty, however tactless. "I'd been doing these puzzles for a while, but you brought me to a whole new level," he told Liza.

"I guess so, if you could come up with a sudoku using only the bare minimum of clues," she replied.

"I hope you'll check it out for me," Dalen said.

"Definitely," Liza promised. "Good luck on the outside."

"Thanks." Dalen went back to his faux German accent. "Perhaps I giff you a call on der telefunken."

With that, a guard arrived at the classroom door to lead the students back into their prison routine. Liza collected her stuff, and then another guard escorted her and Kevin down the corridors and through a series of gates.

An assistant warden met them just before they exited. "It was a small sample group, but everyone seemed pretty enthusiastic about your class," he said. "I understand that you'll be very busy. Do you think you could come up with a curriculum that would work with the general prison population?"

"I think it would definitely run longer, with more time introducing the basics," Liza replied, thinking of the steep learning curve Ritz had suffered from. "Some things have to be explained more simply"—in spite of Conn Lezat's penchant for esoteric math—"and the final project probably needs to be broken down into easier stages."

After all, only Fat Frankie and Chris Dalen had even managed to create a sudoku, and Basso had raised some valid concerns about accomplishing that.

The three made some agreeable noises at each other, and Liza and Kevin finally got outside.

Liza released a long breath that came out as a plume of condensation in the cold air. She was a little surprised it didn't come out gray. The longer she stayed in the prison, the more she felt as if she were inhaling air that every other inmate had already breathed.

She shivered, but that wasn't all reaction. The day was bright and clear—probably a peculiar form of torture for the people who couldn't just walk out the prison gates. But it was really *cold*.

That was one of the more perverse twists of Oregon winter weather. The damp, cloudy, gray days usually had more moderate temperatures than days with clear skies. Then, apparently, any warmth seemed to escape into outer space or something.

Juggling an attaché case and shoulder bag, Liza struggled to zip up her Eddie Bauer parka, something she had neglected to do while still inside. She was so distracted trying to insert the tab in the zipper that she almost collided with someone heading from the parking area toward the gate.

Liza stepped back, recognizing the round face wreathed about with a hand-knitted scarf. "Why, Mrs. H.—what brings you out here?"

Mrs. Halvorsen was Liza's next-door neighbor. Growing up in the small-town ambience of Maiden's Bay, Liza had looked on the older woman as a sort of surrogate grandmother, enjoying milk and cookies in her kitchen. Since returning to her old hometown, Liza found her neighbor treating her to glasses of fairly dreadful sherry while trying to hook her up in a series of matchmaking attempts.

Today, she thought, Mrs. H.'s usually cheerful face looked more disconcerted than anything else. "I'm here doing my Christian duty," she finally replied.

"Oh," Liza said brilliantly. Well, Mrs. H. could usually be found reading an enormous family Bible—although her interpretations could be pretty surprising. Mrs. H. beat her arms against herself, in spite of being fairly bundled up. Liza suddenly felt guilty, looking at her neighbor's wan face. "You should go inside and warm up."

With a quick nod to Kevin, Mrs. H. hurried over to the gate. Kevin looked over his shoulder as he walked with Liza to his big, black SUV. The thing bulked over most of the vehicles in the parking area, including some sort of repair truck. "Funny," he said, "Mrs. H. is usually a lot more chatty."

"I guess she's doing some kind of Bible class with the inmates." Liza frowned, recalling the look on Mrs. H.'s face. "I wish I'd known. We could have offered her a lift."

"A lift?" Kevin said. "That's awfully generous—with my car."

"Mrs. H. could use a little friendly help," Liza told him. "That huge, ancient Oldsmobile she drives isn't great when it comes to MPGs. And you know what gas costs these days."

Kevin looked at her. "A lot of people are feeling that pinch."

"Mrs. H. is feeling it a bit worse, I'd say," Liza went on. "Her husband's company rejiggered their pension plan."

Kevin's breath came out in a white puff. "That can't be good."

"Especially for mere surviving spouses. Her monthly income took a nasty hit." Liza paused. "And you remember that storm a couple of weeks ago?"

Kevin nodded. "We lost a tree on the inn property."

"The same thing happened on Hackleberry Avenue—except the top of the tree landed in Mrs. H.'s living room. Luckily it was at the end of the storm, so the furnishings weren't ruined. But when she went to her insurance company to pay for repairs, they lowballed all the costs."

That stopped Kevin with his key halfway to the SUV door lock. "They screwed her over?"

Liza nodded. "Big time. She got a policy years ago with the Western Assurance Group."

"The people with all those ads on TV saying, 'Rest assured?' " Kevin asked.

"Those are the ones. Well, Mrs. H. kept paying the same premiums, but the company kept sneaking in changes to the terms—changes that shrank the coverage considerably."

Kevin's eyebrows rose. "Makes me want to check my own homeowner's policy."

"Tell me about it," Liza said. "Since Mom passed away, I've just kept paying the premiums on her policy for the house. Now I'll have to dig out all her old paperwork and compare what she bought—and what I've got now."

She shook her head. "In the meantime, Mrs. H. has plastic wrapped around one side of her house, and she'll have to pay about half of what the repairs will cost."

"So she takes a hit both in her income and in her savings." Kevin opened the door then went round to the driver's side of the SUV.

"Not only that, but there's talk of raising the tax assessments in our neighborhood. We're too close to those pricey developments that sprang up on the outskirts of town," Liza said.

"You mean 'Little California?' " Kevin asked with a grin.

"As if you never get any Californians over at the Killamook Inn," Liza said, climbing aboard.

"Yeah, but they don't decide to live there."

The influx of Californian money had brought a latte place and several high-style boutiques to Maiden's Bay. This new development, however, was alarming.

"Seriously, though," Liza said. "If property taxes go up, Mrs. H. may not be able to afford her home. I still have some public relations money coming in from my partnership in Markson Associates and now the syndication of my column. What's she going to do?"

Kevin shrugged as he settled in behind the wheel. "Didn't you mention that she had Michael painting and redoing the spare bedroom to pay his keep while he was staying here? Maybe Mrs. H. is going into the bed-and-breakfast business."

"I hadn't thought of that," Liza said with a frown.

"You don't have to worry," Kevin assured her. "I'm not afraid of the competition."

"I'm just worried about how much business she'd get," Liza said. "Maiden's Bay isn't exactly what you'd call a hot destination."

She was interrupted by a tap on her window—make that more like insistent rapping.

Liza turned to find a short man in a brown polyester parka right out of the seventies peering in at her. He had a face like an old basset hound, all jowls and wrinkles. But instead of that breed's usual lugubrious expression, this guy reminded Liza of the aggressive little schnauzer belonging to one of her aunts. The mutt considered every visitor an intolerable provocation to be greeted with snarls and snaps.

In this case, the aggression came out in raps.

It took a moment to locate the button that lowered the window. "What's your problem," Liza asked.

Mr. Hound Dog thrust his pink, saggy face into the opening. "You're Liza Kelly—the one teaching that sudoku class." The words came out more like an accusation than a question.

Not a fan, I suspect, Liza thought. "I am," she said aloud. "Who are you?"

"Howard Frost, Western Assurance Group."

"Why doesn't that reassure me?" Liza asked, thinking about Mrs. H.'s payment problems.

"My company held the policy for *Composition in Blue, Red, and Green.*" Seeing Liza's look of incomprehension, the insurance man added, "The Mondrian that Christopher Dalen stole."

"Oh," Liza said, "I can't say we ever talked about that."

"But he did class work for you?" Frost pressed. "You should understand that that prisoner is not allowed any communication, written or otherwise—"

"He's getting released today!" Liza burst out.

"—to ensure he cannot pass information regarding the present location of the artwork he stole," Frost continued inexorably.

Liza blinked. "You think he's making secret messages in sudoku puzzles?" She dug into her attaché case and pulled out a copy of Chris Dalen's seventeen-clue wonder. "Here you go—knock yourself out."

Crumpling the paper, Liza tucked it down the front of Howard Frost's parka. Then she turned to Kevin. "Let's get out of here."

3

As they drove off, Liza caught a glimpse of Howard Frost in the side mirror. He'd spread out the paper with the sudoku, perusing the puzzle as if it held the secrets of the ages.

"What do you think that was about?" Kevin asked.

"I guess the Western Assurance Group may get away with stiffing smaller clients," Liza said. "But the painting Chris Dalen stole left them on the hook for at least a couple of million. Even after a dozen years, they must have some flunky out trying to recover it."

"Good luck with that," Kevin said with a smile. "So, shall I drop you at the *Oregon Daily*, or do you want to stop off at Ma's Café for a bite to eat?"

Liza grinned back. "What? Spoil my appetite for dinner tonight?"

"And here I thought you were just coming for the ambience."

The Killamook Inn had a deserved reputation for its kitchen. And when Kevin invited her to the dining room, he always reserved table twenty-one, the quiet, romantic table in the corner that every good dining establishment should have.

"Nope, definitely the food," Liza assured Kevin.

Well, he didn't take it personally. Instead, Kevin laughed all the way to the satellite office of the *Oregon Daily*. Actually, that was a pretty grandiose title for an operation shoehorned into the second floor of a strip mall outside of town. Lately, Liza had found herself spending a lot of time there with Ava as the launch date for her syndicated column came closer.

Liza transferred to her car, waved good-bye to Kevin, and drove off toward Hackleberry Avenue and home. Turning onto her block, she saw Mrs. H.'s house half wrapped in plastic and sighed.

But her mood lifted as she pulled into her driveway. The sound of her engine brought a reddish-furred head poking up in the front window. Then barking erupted as she put her key in the lock. Rusty danced around the living room as Liza came in. The dog's coloring came from his Irish setter ancestry. As for his perpetual good humor, that probably came from the mutt side of his parentage. Shortly after moving back to Maiden's Bay, Liza had found the dog wandering the neighborhood. She'd named him Rusty and taken him in to lighten the mood in her old family homestead.

And Rusty did his best to oblige, like his cheerful greeting. He also deftly sidestepped while he moved around, leading them toward the kitchen counter where the jar containing his dog treats reposed.

Rusty paused, looking up at Liza expectantly.

She laughed, opening the jar. "Knock it off, you fraud." He caught the treat on the fly, ran in a victory circle, and settled down contentedly in a patch of sunshine from the window.

Liza took a seat at the kitchen table and fished a copy of Chris Dalen's puzzle out of her attaché. As she worked her way through the grid, she shook her head. Minimum sudoku represented a specialized province in Sudoku Nation. In fact, Liza knew of a website that collected all known seventeen-clue puzzles.

She frowned as she worked toward a solution. In the early days of sudoku, people believed the fewer the clues, the more difficult the puzzle. Actually, many minimal puzzles tended to the easier side of the spectrum, solvable with simpler techniques.

The puzzle at hand was a bit more complicated than that. She compared her solution to the one Chris Dalen had given her. They matched.

Liza leaned back in her chair. Hmmm. Maybe this was the seed of a new column, about puzzle construction or the minimum number of clues necessary to make a valid sudoku. Michelle Markson would love to see a column come out of the prison class—she'd probably want all the celebrity names mentioned. Too bad Ritz Tarleton hadn't come up with it. Michelle would insist that Liza name it after the girl, like Bowman's Bingo.

Well, Chris managed a pretty impressive achievement, Liza told herself. *Maybe I could call it "Dalen's enigma."*

But even as she considered the idea, niggling doubts appeared in the back of her head. Liza glanced over at her computer, ensconced in the corner of the living room she'd converted into a makeshift office. Maybe she should check that minimum sudoku site. What if Chris had just copied a puzzle from there and passed it off as his own?

Liza sat down at the keyboard, then hesitated again. Chris had told her that he wasn't allowed access to a computer. Then a sarcastic voice began speaking up in the back of her head. *Right. And we should believe him because he's an art thief and, up to this morning, an imprisoned felon.*

She started going online, then canceled that. She wasn't going to waste time checking on Chris Dalen's honesty. Nor was she going to unleash "Dalen's enigma" upon the world. It was a cool title, but this was just a seventeen-clue puzzle—interesting, but not earthshaking.

Instead, Liza called up the Solv-a-doku program on her computer and used it to check whether the minimal puzzle was a true sudoku with only one possible solution. It was. Nodding, Liza saved the puzzle, then called up one she was still working on. This was a killer sudoku that had, on and off, taken several days of construction. As Liza worked her way into it again, time quietly slipped by.

The sudden bleating of the telephone came as a shock. Liza turned away from the computer screen to see that the spot of light from the window had shifted considerably. It had also become a lot less bright.

She picked up the handset. "Hello?"

"I've been cooling my heels in a reception area while some studio small fry tries to convince me he's a big shot," Michael Langley's voice came over the line. He'd been staying with Mrs. H. until a desperate request for his script-doctoring services had taken him back to Hollywood. "Anyway, they've got a flatscreen TV up on the wall—probably worth more than they'll pay me on this gig—and the weather report is talking about nasty weather up your way."

Liza frowned. "That offshore storm? I thought that was supposed to hit us sometime late tomorrow."

"Well, it looks as though the schedule has moved up—unlike the project I'm stuck with." Exasperation put a slight edge into her almost ex-husband's voice, but that quickly moderated into concern. "They're talking about snow and wind and all sorts of unpleasantness overnight. Are you going to be okay?"

"It won't be the first time something like that has happened around Maiden's Bay," Liza said. "Just about every winter, some kind of squall comes in, knocks down a few trees or utility poles, and we lose power for a while. You know, just like the brushfires, earthquakes, mudslides, and whatnot that you enjoy down south."

Michael chuckled. "I think you left out crime waves, riots,

and civil disobedience." Then the concern came back. "You're going to be all right, though?"

"It gets to be second nature," she assured him. "We make sure there are lots of batteries for the radio, candles and lanterns, and everybody runs to the store to buy up all the bread and milk. I should probably make sure I've got a good supply of Rusty's food." Her dog's head came up off the rug, hearing his name and the word "food" in the same sentence.

"I sort of ignored you up there most of last winter." That had been the really rough time after they had just split. Liza remembered it as a long, lonely, gray time. "I just—I didn't want to do that again," Michael said.

"Well, I suppose I should thank you," Liza told him. "I've been working on a puzzle and haven't heard any new reports on the TV or radio."

"Then that's a good thing." Michael laughed. "When you get your teeth into a sudoku, you wouldn't notice if the front window blew out until the snow was drifting around your feet."

"Maybe," she retorted. "But I'm not the one who got so wound up in a fiendish sudoku that he let a pot not only boil empty, but actually melt on our stove."

Michael harrumphed, but he couldn't deny his own sudoku fanaticism. "I just wanted to make sure you'd be okay, safe at home tonight."

"I'll be fine." Liza didn't want to tell Michael about her dinner date with Kevin, so she resorted to a little verbal sidestep. "I suppose I should get moving to the store now. Tell you what, I'll call you in the morning and tell you how much snow I have to shovel."

"Fine." Michael lowered his voice. "The way things are going, I could still be sitting around here."

They exchanged good-byes and Liza hung up, sending a guilty look toward Rusty. "Well, come on. We might as well go to the store and make some part of what I said true."

She got the leash. Rusty enjoyed the walk to Castelli's Market, sniffing the air appreciatively. Liza was less cheerful. The air was still cold, but she could feel the trace of dampness in it that predicted—or was that threatened?—future snow.

Liza left Rusty outside and braved quite a crowd at Castelli's to pick up her snow supplies. Arriving back home, she had to drop her shopping sacks and run to the phone without even opening her coat. Rusty ran around, trailing his leash and barking as the phone continued to bleat.

Shushing the dog, Liza picked up the receiver while fighting pangs of conscience. Michael had a writer's ear—not to mention a mystery writer's suspicious mind. Had he detected some trace of ambivalence in her voice—and rung back to call her on it?

"Hey, Liza," Kevin's voice came over the line. "I don't know if you've been catching the weather report—"

"I got some warning," Liza replied, diplomatically avoiding any mention of her source. "In fact, I just got back from carting in the emergency provisions."

"Speaking of which," Kevin began.

Liza sighed, wondering if he was going to call the evening off.

"My chef is in the middle of creating some special lamb thing for tonight, just for you," Kevin said. "But I think we ought to get together a little earlier than we planned."

"Sounds like a good idea," Liza admitted.

"Fine. I'll pick you up in say . . . three hours?" Kevin said. "You make jokes about my SUV, but I think it's better in case of rough weather."

Liza checked the wall clock—five minutes before Kevin was supposed to arrive. Then she took a last-minute look in her mirror. She was wearing the Armani suit she'd picked up on Rodeo Drive during that last wild visit to L.A. solving

Derrick Robbins's murder. The suit had knocked a pretty good dent into her credit balance, but had been necessary—business camouflage.

Now it was the newest, nicest suit in her wardrobe. The charcoal gray wool complemented the wine-colored sweater she was wearing underneath. As for the rest, she had the regulation number of eyes, nostrils . . .

Liza parted her lips—nothing stuck in her teeth. Her shoulder-length hair, dark brown with hints of chestnut, fell naturally. Liza hadn't fooled with it. Frankly, she needed a trim. That brought up an unwelcome image of Michael, whose untidy curls always seemed to need cutting. Liza repressed that thought and pulled on her good dress coat.

"Probably smarter to bring my Eddie Bauer special," she muttered, flicking a bit of dog hair off the cashmere. The clouds had gathered threateningly, and from the sound of things, the wind was picking up.

It wasn't howling quite yet, but Rusty had already taken what Liza considered his storm station, squirming in behind the sofa.

"I left you some extra dry food," Liza told her dog. "Don't make a pig of yourself. With this weather, it may have to last you till morning."

She'd also taken the precaution of spreading newspapers across the kitchen's linoleum floor.

Well, I've said it out loud, she thought, turning to the door as she heard Kevin's big behemoth pulling up in her driveway. "Take it easy, Rusty," she said. "I should be home in a little while." All she got was a muffled *woof* from under the couch.

Outside it was still cold, and that "snow is on the way" dampness just about smacked her in the face, backed up by an insistent breeze. Besides cutting right through her dressy clothes, it also blew her hair all over the place.

"You look great," Kevin said, rushing over to give her his arm.

"I look like Cousin It from *The Addams Family*," Liza groused, tucking her arm through the crook of his elbow and huddling close, trying to use him as a windbreak.

Flipping down the vanity mirror on her side, she tried to repair the damage as Kevin drove along the coastal highway toward the inn. Branches on the evergreens were already whipping around. The water of Killamook Bay looked as if it had been transformed to lead, except for the whitecaps lashed up by the now howling wind.

Snow began falling when they were about three-quarters of the way there. And this wasn't the cute, lacey variety. No, these snowflakes were little white pellets that struck the rear windshield like tiny machine gun bullets.

"I hope you don't take offense," Liza told Kevin, "but I think the sooner we finish supper, the better."

A sort of rough-hewn porte cochere protected them from the buffeting wind when they pulled up at the Killamook Inn's main building. Kevin let one of the valets take his SUV and ushered Liza inside. The reception area was large, rustic, and blessedly warm. They had just stepped onto a rich length of carpeting on their way to the dining room when the assistant manager came rushing over from behind the reception desk.

"Er, Kevin, we've got someone who registered—kind of a special guest—he'd like to meet with you, discuss the operation." Kevin's usually unflappable assistant looked as if his blazer didn't fit right. He handed over a business card. Liza craned her head to get a look.

"Frederick 'Fritz' Tarleton, Tarleton Tours," she read aloud. "Father of our little Ritz, I suppose."

"Head of one of the biggest high-end tourism outfits in the country." Kevin glanced from the card to Liza and actually bit his lip. Liza could see the conflict—business versus having a personal life. If he sat down in the dining room with Tarleton, he lost his time with Liza, and maybe the wonderful lamb dish if the big shot was demanding enough.

With a quick glance at his watch, Kevin asked, "Where is Mr. Tarleton?"

"In his room," the assistant replied.

Kevin nodded. "Let's see if I can catch him there." He turned to Liza. "Would you mind waiting a little bit?"

"Hey, in my previous life, that was part of the job description," she assured him. She left Kevin, who walked back to the reception area with his number-two man while shooting his sleeves—Kevin's equivalent of girding his loins for business battle.

Liza went to the dining room entrance and checked her coat. Glancing into the large room, she saw only a couple of tables occupied. The oversized fireplace in the far wall held an enormous log surrounded by kindling, but it hadn't been lit yet.

"Not enough of an audience for the floor show," she muttered. Well, that was the way Kevin described the nightly fireplace ritual.

The maitre d' approached with his usual effusive greeting, and Liza raised both hands. "Kevin has to take care of something," she said. "I think I'll wait in the bar." Liza managed to sidestep into the bar, preventing the man from turning her arrival into an "entrance." The long, dimly lit room also had customers, people enjoying predinner drinks or looking for some cocktail camaraderie.

She avoided the bar itself, heading to the row of tables down the wall where she hoped to find an inconspicuous seat. The farther along she got, the dimmer the lights became. Liza stopped, resting her hand on the back of a seat.

"Sorry," a strangely familiar voice told her. "This one is occupied." Liza peered into the shadows. Then her eyes went big in surprise.

"Chris Dalen!" she burst out in surprise. "What the hell are you doing here?"

4

For a second, Dalen looked as surprised as Liza when she sat down at the table. Then his lips quirked in a crooked smile. "Und zo, ve meet again," he said in his hokey German accent. With his next words, he switched back to his normal voice. "I suppose I shouldn't be shocked, considering that your friend Kevin runs this joint."

"I'm not sure he'd appreciate you calling this a joint," Liza said.

"I expect not," Dalen replied. "Well, it sure beats hell out of the joint where I've spent the last dozen or so years. Nicer dress code, for one thing." He fingered the lapel on the suit he was wearing. It was a little too narrow to be fashionable, maybe ten or twelve years out of style. Back then, though, it had been a good, expensive suit.

Now it hung on Dalen's emaciated frame. Liza figured he could fit two fingers under the collar of his dress shirt. "That's all very interesting," she said. "But it still doesn't answer my question about what you're doing here."

Dalen shrugged, rattling the ice in his highball glass. "Guess I was looking for a place where I could order top-shelf booze, enjoy a room where *I* get to lock the door, and sleep in a comfortable bed with a blanket that doesn't rasp the skin off me. I wanted one taste of the old, good life." He lapsed back into his fractured German shtick. "Und tomorrow, I get on der telefunken und call mein zister."

His crooked grin came back. "I'll bunk in her spare room, find a nice job filling ice cream cones or something, and lead a good, gray life."

Liza looked at him for a long moment. "And the fact that Ritz Tarleton's father just happens to be here this evening is a complete coincidence?"

Dalen's face barely changed. "Oh, you heard Daddy was in the building? Well, maybe the kid mentioned something about that . . ."

"You're trying to sell off that painting to him."

Chris Dalen dropped the ironic pose like a mask. "I know you've gotten involved in a couple of police cases. But you're still pretty much a civilian, so I'll be straight with you. I haven't got much time left. Everybody who knows about the Mondrian sees me as one big dollar sign, and after those butcher-doctors in the joint were done with me, I was left in no shape to defend myself. As our pal Mr. Lezat might say, best to relieve myself of a major liability."

Liza blinked. "You make it sound like you're in danger."

"Hey, Mr. Tarleton Tours is probably the gentleman of the bunch," Dalen said. "Think of Fat Frankie Basso. There's a guy who indulges his appetites for more than just food. He's probably more used to moving the contents of knocked-over warehouses, but if he could make a connection to sell the Mondrian for half or even a third of its real value, that would still be more than a million bucks in his pocket, just for getting his hands on the painting."

Dalen gave a bitter laugh. "And what is it? The damned thing looks like a schematic for a tile bathroom floor. A buck two-eighty's worth of paint on canvas, but people who know squat about art will pay three mill for it on some expert's say-so. Now, if I had boosted the *Mona Lisa* . . ."

His humor suddenly vanished. "But this is just business—maybe dangerous enough that it's not a good idea to be seen talking with me." With that, Dalen got up and left the table.

Liza sat where she was, and a moment later a waiter came by to take her order. "Er, the gentleman said you were picking up his tab."

"Then I guess I am." Liza ordered a glass of red wine. It arrived in a tall stemmed glass, and Liza swirled the red liquid around, wondering how much of what Dalen had said was for real, and how much was the newly freed man's sense of humor.

Liza tried to nurse her drinks, but she'd gotten through three large glasses of wine by the time Kevin finally rejoined her. She squinted at her watch. "I think we're just about where we'd be if we hadn't tried starting off early."

Kevin raised his hands as if he were surrendering. "I'm really sorry. But this is a big deal, Liza. Tarleton had all sorts of questions about the inn. He covered everything—"

"Including, maybe, his ass," Liza put in. While Kevin stared at her, she told him about her conversation with Chris Dalen.

"I hate to burst your bubble, but I think you're being used as a cover for Fritz Tarleton making a deal with Dalen over that missing picture."

Seeing the look on his face, she stretched out a hand, contrite. "Damn, I'm sorry. That didn't sound quite as nasty when it was in my head."

Kevin's expression smoothed away into a stern mask—his "I'm thinking" face.

"What they're doing—that's criminal conspiracy, isn't it?" Liza noticed she had a little trouble getting "criminal conspiracy" out clearly.

"Either way, I wouldn't want to kill any chance of the inn becoming a Tarleton destination." Kevin spoke sourly. "It's nothing to do with us. Let's just forget it."

They headed back to the dining room, which had filled a bit more. The big log in the fireplace was now crackling with flames that danced wildly in time to the wind howling over and sometimes through the chimney.

"Sounds great out there," Liza said.

Kevin nodded. "We've got a coating already, and the reports just seem to be getting worse."

Even so, she couldn't bring herself to wolf her way through the meal that Rocco the chef sent out to their quiet table in the corner. The lamb wasn't just fork-tender, it seemed to part when Liza breathed on it. It was the real thing, young and succulent, in a sauce that mixed some sort of potent potable—cognac, maybe—with a variety of herbs. Liza could recognize rosemary, but there were a lot of other condiments. The whole thing came on a bed of incredibly thin, small *pommes frites*, crunchier than french fries but not as crispy as potato sticks. With glazed fresh vegetables, and a dessert of sinful chocolate cake with hot brandied chocolate sauce—not to mention another bottle of good red wine—conversation tended to be on the sparse side.

After all, it's bad manners to talk with your mouth full.

"It's a funny thing," Kevin said, wiping his lips with his napkin. "I always thought Chris Dalen was the only honest one in your class."

That almost sent a sip of wine the wrong way—out Liza's nose. "How do you figure that?"

"Conn Lezat still won't admit to any wrongdoing. He calls the nonsense he pulled while wrecking his company 'nonviable business strategies.'" Kevin shook his head. "I'm not sure whether it's the strategy or the business that was nonviable."

Liza nodded. "And I suppose Frankie Basso uses 'unorthodox business methods.'"

"Fat Frankie would never say that—but he does believe he's a businessman," Kevin said. "As for Ritz Tarleton, I'm not sure if she rates as a socialite or a sociopath. She really seems to have a hard time understanding why those no-body little police people insist on trying to keep her from doing whatever the hell she wants."

"And Chris?" Liza asked.

"He was up front from the first day of class. He stole something and got put away for it."

Liza laughed. "Here's to Chris Dalen—the honest crook." She raised her glass as Kevin's assistant manager came up to the table, a worried expression on his face.

"All the rest of tonight's dinner reservations have been canceled. Rocco's suggesting that we close the kitchen and let his staff make it home while they still can."

"Do it," Kevin said, his expression losing several shades of cheerfulness.

"Well, at least it wasn't Mr. Tarleton with a demand for an elephant-ear sandwich." Liza put her hand to her mouth. "Oh, that was miserable. I don't even know why I said that."

"I think you were trying to be funny," Kevin said.

"I don't like the way that Tarleton guy made you jump through hoops."

"Not much choice involved for me," Kevin said. "I knew coming in that this was a responsible job."

"Yeah, I used to have a job like that," Liza joked feebly. "Whenever anything went wrong, I was responsible."

"That's kind of the way I feel about this place," Kevin told her, "except I call it 'the buck stops here.' "

He leaned forward, spreading his hands. "When I did the hunting and fishing guide thing, I was pretty much a lone wolf. Even when I got married and Josette came in with me, it was a family business at best."

"Until your wife got tired of living out of sleeping bags," Liza said.

Kevin nodded. "After I went back to school and took the job here, I realized that it was more than being responsible for running a good operation. I had a responsibility to the team I created. I recruited Rocco from culinary school to come up with a new menu and ramrod the kitchens. This place was a glorified fishing camp when I came here. I saw that we needed more than good guides. So I hired and trained people, arranged deep-sea charters with some of the fishermen at Maiden's Bay, added a business conference center for the off-season, a spa that I hope to enlarge—"

"You've got ambitions," Liza said.

"And I've got responsibilities—to the people who own the inn and to the people who work here. The right word from Tarleton and his company could put us on the map, nationally, even internationally." Kevin's expression darkened. "Or he could hurt us. He's the guy who rates resorts. I'm just the guy doing the best he can here. If Tarleton talked to the owners about going in a new direction—"

That would probably translate into new management, Liza silently finished for him.

The silence they sat in had nothing to do with good food. Then, with an obvious intention of changing the subject, Kevin said, "You know, the weather is getting even worse than the forecasters expected. Maybe you should stay tonight. The next thing you know, we're going to have trees down and the power out—"

As if on cue, the whole room went dark. The only illumination came from the leaping flames in the fireplace and the small candles on each table.

Kevin jumped to his feet. "Nothing to worry about, folks. We have our own generator." A moment later, the subdued dining room lighting came back. Liza squinted. Was it her imagination, or did it seem more subdued than usual?

Intentional or not, that blink of the lights seemed to signal "last call" to the diners. They had all reached the dessert and after-dinner drinks stage anyway. And except for Liza, they were all guests at the inn. The bartender and maitre d', it turned out, had already arranged to bunk at the inn.

Liza smiled ruefully. *I guess everybody else got out while the going was still good.*

Kevin sat back at the table. "We can put you up in cabin one," he said. "It's nearby . . . and discreet."

I guess he wouldn't want to advertise that he's putting his girlfriend up in a room, Liza thought. "Thanks," she said.

Further conversation was interrupted by the approach of Kevin's assistant. He'd already ditched his blazer in favor of a waxed weatherproof coat.

"We'll have to make a quick check of the property." Kevin looked down at his suit. "I'd better change into something a little less formal. I'll leave you with John. He'll make all the arrangements."

Those arrangements took a bit longer than Liza might have expected. The cabin was all ready for occupation. The problem was getting Liza out to it. John finally dug up a hooded rubber slicker and boots used by the maids in inclement weather. The pull-on boots weren't made to accommodate heels, and Liza's stocking-clad feet swam around in them.

That wasn't so bad indoors, but it made the footing considerably worse when she and John stepped outside into what had become a howling blizzard. She had to watch where she put her feet in the deepening snow while making sure the wind didn't snatch away her suddenly billowing raingear or yank away the hood to dump a quart or two of snow down her neck. The snow and wind combination felt more like a sandblasting abrasive than weather.

John took one arm, and Liza used the other to hold the raincoat to her as they made it to the barely seen bulk of the cabin in a sort of hunchbacked stagger. Handing Liza the LED lantern he'd been carrying, John unlocked the door and unceremoniously got them inside. Liza raised the lantern while using her other hand to try and rub some life back into her stinging face.

She'd been in the cabins at the Killamook Inn before. They offered a strange blend of rustic and ritzy. Dark-paneled walls and beams were decorated with tasteful examples of native and local art. A deep-pile rug soothed once you got past the mudroom in the entranceway. Besides pegs for hanging clothes—which Liza used immediately for her now-streaming slicker—the entrance also offered racks for guns or fishing rods.

John had already scraped his feet and headed straight for the big fireplace. The makings of a small inferno were in it, only waiting for a match. By the time Liza got free of her flapping galoshes, a cheerful blaze was adding light and warmth to the room.

The assistant manager met her, rubbing his hands together as she came into the room. "I'll leave the lantern with you, the batteries have been fully charged. And there are candles and oil lamps here as well."

"That's about as good as I could expect things to be if the power went out at home," Liza told him. "Thanks."

He nodded. "I'd just be—um, sparing—with electric lights right now. We've got the generator—"

"But that's for essential services. I understand." Liza stifled a yawn. "Besides, I'll probably be turning in."

John nodded again. "Anything you need, just pick up the phone. You've got a secure connection to the reception desk—we ran the phone lines from the cabins underground. As for outside calls, that will be up to what the storm brings down. I'm sure Kevin will stop by to see you after we've made the rounds."

Liza thanked John and saw him to the door. They both nearly got flattened opening the damned thing, and Liza had to shove it closed against that insistent wind. Then she went back to the fire to warm up.

That bed was looking better by the moment. In keeping with the setting, it was a faux antique solid mahogany sled style. But the square yardage on the thing was probably half the size of the studio apartment Liza had rented on first coming to L.A.

They must have laid two super-kingsize mattresses together, she thought, hauling back the thick but feather-weight comforters. Beneath were an enormous striped Hudson Bay–style wool blanket and crisp cotton sheets.

For a moment, Liza thought longingly of the bag of overnight necessities she always kept packed . . . in the trunk of her car back at home. "I guess no jammies tonight," she murmured.

She was halfway out of her Armani jacket when she remembered John's words. "I'm sure Kevin will stop by to see you . . ."

A jumble of thoughts ran through her head. A delicious dinner, lots of wine, a romantic snowbound cabin—was tonight going to be The Night? Back in high school, he'd made his big move after taking Liza to dinner at the fanciest place in Maiden's Bay, Fruit of the Sea. Was history about to repeat itself?

Maybe it was wishful thinking or a tipsy whim. But when Liza plunged under the covers, everything she'd been wearing sat neatly folded on the top of the long dresser beside the bed.

Liza moved quickly—even with the fire going, it was *chilly* in the cabin! She crawled toward the middle of the bed and huddled in on herself, trying to get warm.

"Silly," she scolded herself. "By the time Kevin gets here—if he gets here—you'll probably be snoring so loud, you'll drown out the sound of his knock."

But her eyes didn't shut, and she didn't drift off. She lay carefully listening for anything over the screaming of the wind. Suppose Kevin came in to make a grand gesture? Liza imagined him walking in, wreathed with snow, a thermos of Rocco's wonderful coffee in one hand and a bottle of brandy in the other.

Or maybe . . . she'd always teased him about the big bearskin rug on the floor of his office, a relic of his grandfather's hunting prowess. Suppose he came in with a bottle of brandy and *that*?

Liza giggled. They could spread it out right over the bed . . .

She reached out with a smoothing gesture, and that's

when she felt the hand. Liza poked around, realizing she was right at the junction of the two mattresses. The hand was under the bottom sheet on the bed. She poked again. It was under the mattress pad.

"Of all the silly . . ." she muttered. Was this the reason for the holdup in getting her out here? Trying to pop out of the bed didn't seem like much of a grand gesture to her. More like the kind of stunt a high school sophomore might pull to scare his girlfriend.

"I know you're in there," Liza said, prodding at Kevin's hand.

It didn't move.

"Come on!" Liza's anger slowly turned to concern. Burying himself under all this stuff, had Kevin smothered himself?

She jumped off the mattress, tearing at the bedclothes. Comforter, blanket, top sheet, all went flying. The fitted sheet at the bottom was more of struggle, as was the mattress pad. Finally Liza managed to pull them loose. Now she could see the hand sticking up between the mattresses.

"Kevin, come *on*!" she grunted, hauling at the side of a mattress. "If this was ever funny, it stopped being that a long time ago." The mattress finally shifted, nearly sending Liza back on her behind. She set off crawling across the yielding surface, debating whether she should throttle Kevin or start CPR.

Liza finally reached the gap she'd created . . . and suddenly found it very hard to breathe. Kevin wasn't down there, tucked into the bed.

Instead, she found herself staring into the lifeless eyes of Chris Dalen.

5

"Holy jumping Judas Priest!" Liza didn't remember crossing the expanse of mattress. All of a sudden she was standing on the plush carpeting, one big mass of gooseflesh—and not just from the chill air.

First she had to think past her brain's reflexive chattering of "Dead body! Dead body!" Okay. There was a dead body. Somebody had created it and put it there. Was this person still around? The logic was pretty grim. If the killer was in the cabin, it was a little late to try playing dumb. Not after tearing the bed apart and screaming like a banshee while she rocketed out of the covers.

For a second, Liza shot a yearning look at her clothes neatly arrayed on the dresser. Of all the outfits she'd prefer to wear while dealing with a hiding murderer, her birthday suit was not at the top of the list. Of course, she'd prefer not to be in this situation at all. Not that anyone had ever asked her opinion about it.

She ran the mental image of the late Chris Dalen through her memory, stifling another shudder.

No blood.

That realization sent her sprinting to the cabin's kitchenette. It wasn't up to Rocco's feast production center, but it did have lots of cooking tools—and she would feel a lot better holding a carving knife right now.

Liza grabbed the biggest blade she could and turned to face the room. As far as she could see, there were no knives missing. She leaned back against the under-counter fridge—too small for someone to hide in—and promptly jumped as the cold metal goosed her bare bottom.

She glared into the far corners of the cabin. The white glow of the LED lantern didn't reach very far, and the flickering firelight made shadows leap and jitter at the edges of the room. With the lantern in one hand (ready to throw) and the knife in the other (ready to stab), Liza ensured that they were just shadows, not murderers.

Next stop, the bathroom—nobody there, either, not even in the shower.

Liza grabbed the first thing her hand landed on—a towel—and headed straight for the telephone.

"C'mon, c'mon, work," she muttered as she picked up the handset. She'd seen this scene in too many horror movies . . . Liza sighed with relief when she got a dial tone. She glanced at the card around the phone's keypad and stabbed down on the buttons that contacted the reception desk.

"Killamook Inn," a familiar voice answered—the bartender?

Guess he's doing extra duty while he stays over, Liza thought.

"This is Liza Kelly in cabin one," she said. "There's a dead body here. I need the cops and Kevin—er, not necessarily in that order."

"Well, the cops are on the way—they rescued a guy walking along the highway, and they're coming here to try warming him up."

"Then get them over here—and Kevin, too," Liza added. She shook out the towel, wrapped it around herself, and stared downward in dismay. It didn't quite wrap.

"I don't believe this," she muttered. The Killamook Inn boasted the world's largest, most luxurious towels. You could make a damned tent from one of them. So what had she gotten? A hand towel? A washcloth?

Liza had started back to the bathroom when heavy hands began knocking on the cabin door. She whipped around, pulling the towelette up in front of her. If she clamped it under her arms, the terry cloth just covered her front—with maybe a few inches to spare. She didn't want to think what the rear view looked like as she walked to the door and unlocked it.

Sheriff Clements and Deputy Curt Walters came in, hands on their gun butts. Their eyebrows rose pretty precipitately when they saw Liza.

"He's in the bed," she said.

"Looks like you were—" Curt began.

"I was on it. He was in it. Under it. In the middle." Liza took a long breath, realizing her voice kept getting louder and shriller with each sentence. "He's—he was Chris Dalen, a member of my prison sudoku class. He just got out today, and he was here to celebrate—"

The eyebrows, if possible, rose even higher. "I mean," Liza said, trying to start again, "he was here at the inn to celebrate. I got stuck here because of the snow, and I found him stuck here between the mattresses in the bed." She sidled over and pointed carefully, still keeping the towel clamped in place, toward the disarranged bed.

As Sheriff Clements and Curt headed that way, the door swung open again, spraying wind-driven snow and a third person into the room. Liza didn't recognize him. From the meltwater stains up to the knees of his trousers, his sodden dress shoes, and the trench coat clutched around him, the stranger hadn't come out prepared for tonight's weather.

"Liza Kelly, this is Detective Ted Everard of the state police Criminal Investigation Division." A small glint of malice showed in the sheriff's eyes. "I guess you two would have been meeting anyway—the CID sent him out here to look into the sudden rise in major crime statistics here-abouts."

"Forgive me for not shaking hands," Liza said a bit tartly. She had both hands holding down her towel, which showed a distressing tendency to whip in the sudden breeze.

Everard barely glanced at her, occupied as he was in shutting the door. He slung his coat on one of the hooks, revealing an outfit seemingly designed to make people wince—a gray-green suit over a royal blue shirt and a red power tie. The detective moved directly to the bed, where Sheriff Clements was standing.

"Did you know the deceased?" The state cop finally turned to Liza and did a double take. "I guess I can take that as a yes."

"He was my student," Liza protested. A bit belatedly, she remembered all the sniggering jokes about student-teacher relationships on the late-night TV shows. "Come on—he was old enough to be my father, and he had a bad heart."

She realized she was only digging herself in deeper when she heart Curt mutter. "What a way to go."

"Try to think with something north of your belt buckle," Sheriff Clements reproved. "And use your eyes a bit more constructively, too. There's a ligature mark around his neck. He was strangled."

"Look at the wrists." Everard pointed but carefully kept from touching the arm that stuck up. "See the abrasion? He was restrained."

"Kinky," Curt muttered.

"Right," Liza burst out. "We had a wild ride, him com-pletely clothed, and me not. I tied him up, strangled him, and then called the cops dressed only in a little towel. Makes lots of sense, right?"

"Uh . . ." Curt said. "When you put it that way . . ."

"Right," Liza said again. "So could I just get dressed now?"

"I'm afraid this is all part of the crime scene right now," Sheriff Clements told her.

"And I suppose so is the complimentary bathrobe, the other towels, and the slicker hanging by the door." If Liza didn't watch it, her voice was going to start getting loud and shrill again.

"Essentially, yes," the sheriff said.

"Great. Just great." Liza would have liked to start tearing her hair at this point. But then she'd probably lose the towel—and whatever was left of her sanity—altogether.

"I'll survey the crime scene," Everard volunteered. No matter where Liza kept stepping to get out of the way, somehow Everard's survey kept taking him somewhere behind her. She finally planted herself with her back firmly against a blank wall, glaring at the state cop.

Liza was just about to say something when the door opened again. This time Kevin appeared in a waxed coat rimed with snow. After one look and a few words with Clements, he left to reappear with a large trash bag in his hand. It contained a thick terry cloth bathrobe scavenged from another cabin and another one of those slickers the maids used.

"I couldn't find any more galoshes," he said, holding up the slicker while she slipped into the robe. "Guess I'll have to carry you."

That made her fumble as she tried to put on the slicker. "Just don't drop me," she told him as they walked to the door. "Or if you do, try to fix it so I land on my head. I think amnesia would be a good thing about now."

"We will never talk of this," Kevin assured her.

Curt Walters was at least nice enough to open the door for them as Kevin swept her up in his arms and staggered back to the main building. There was one treacherous moment where his foot skidded in snow, but he managed to keep his feet and his hold on Liza.

They entered through the kitchen door. Kevin set Liza down, and she found herself staring as Deputy Brenna Ross and John the assistant manager tended to a shivering figure wrapped up in towels and blankets. A sopping wet brown polyester suit lay on the floor. Brenna and John had the man's hands and feet in pots, carefully letting some water out, then pouring more in.

"Standard procedure to stave off frostbite," Kevin whispered to her. "You've got to bring the temperature in the extremities up slowly to get the blood flowing again." Liza could see what he was talking about when Brenna raised the guy's left hand to put it in a new pot. The skin looked strangely pale—almost waxy.

The stranded motorist winced as his hand went in, even though Liza saw no steam rising from the water. "Compared to how cold he was, that water feels hot," Kevin explained. Liza nodded, looking at the man's face. That was very pale, too, strain pulling the flesh into tight folds.

"Do you recognize him?" she suddenly asked Kevin.

Kevin looked from her to the guy. "Should I?"

"He was at the prison today, in the parking lot."

"The guy from the insurance company?" Kevin obviously had a hard time matching this pale little man with the aggressive figure rapping on his SUV window.

"Howard Frost," Liza said.

Brenna looked up. "That's what his ID says. Apparently he swerved off the road trying to avoid a falling tree about a mile from here. The tree still did a number on his car, and he tried to walk. It's a lucky thing we were coming along behind a road-clearing crew. I don't think he'd have made it."

Liza shuddered, suddenly glad that Kevin's arm was around her. You read about stories like this after every big storm, people found dead in their stranded cars—or outside them. Seeing someone she knew in that situation, even if she didn't like him, made it somehow strike closer to home.

One dead, and one almost, she thought. *That's enough for one night.* All she wanted now was a warm bed and quiet, dreamless sleep.

That's not what she got, though. Sheriff Clements and Detective Everard finished their initial examination of the murder scene, then came to her for a statement. Liza found herself sitting in the guest seat in Kevin's office, glaring at Everard as he paced back and forth over the bearskin rug. *Stupid rug,* she thought. *Stupid cop.*

Clements established himself in the more comfortable chair behind the desk, leaning back and generally saying little. He had mentioned Liza's help in other cases, but that only seemed to inflame Everard's suspicions. "Oh, so this is the 'amateur sleuth' who helped you," he asked.

"That's what the newspapers said," Sheriff Clements replied.

"I don't pay much attention to that nonsense." Everard glanced over at the sheriff. "I also think that professional investigations tend to suffer when amateurs insert themselves. They're either meddlesome idiots who've read too many mystery novels, or publicity hounds."

He paused, turning back to Liza. "I understand you work in the publicity field, Ms. Kelly."

Liza did her best to channel her partner Michelle at her iciest. "I wasn't aware that was something illegal, Detective."

"The fact remains that you were found with the deceased in a state of undress—"

"People usually get undressed when they go to bed. When I did that, I wasn't thinking about playing hostess to a bunch of police—whom, by the way, I had called to the scene." *Note to self,* Liza thought. *Next time you find a dead body in the nude, take the time to get your clothes back on before phoning the cops.*

"After I got to bed, I felt a hand under the covers—under *all* the covers. I had to yank off all the bedclothes and pull the damned bed apart to find Chris Dalen buried under—or between—the mattresses." Liza took a deep breath.

"I was at the inn because Kevin Shepard had invited me to dinner—in fact, he drove me over. But then he was called away on business. While I was waiting, I bumped into Chris Dalen, who intended to spend the evening here."

She went over what Dalen had told her. "I don't know if he actually saw Tarleton—I don't know if anything he told me was true. He could have been amusing himself, yanking my chain. But he suggested he might be in danger because of his hidden painting, and now he's dead."

Everard scowled. "And you didn't think it appropriate to inform the local police about this supposed meeting?"

"As I said, I didn't know if it might be true." Liza gave him a sweet smile. "Then, too, what would the professional investigators do, hearing such a story from a mere amateur sleuth?" Much less flippantly, she added, "Besides, if Sheriff Clements had been involved in a big stakeout here, he may not have found Howard Frost until he'd frozen stiff out on the road."

Everard's blue eyes just about threw sparks, and he clamped his lips so tightly, his slightly lantern jaw quivered. When he recovered himself, he said, "The sheriff may have allowed you some latitude in his investigations. But this case involves the state police."

"I guess so," Clements said amiably, "since a killing and a multimillion-dollar art theft probably shoot our local crime stats even further to hell."

The detective pretended not to hear. "Your attitude and actions create a reasonable suspicion."

"Hey," Liza spoke up, "I didn't have a suspicion I'd be staying here tonight—or that I'd be in cabin one. This isn't exactly the busy season at the Killamook Inn. Whoever stuffed the body in there might have had weeks, even months pass before it was discovered."

"You could have lured Dalen out there," Everard insisted.

"No way to prove that by footprints," the sheriff pointed out. "That wind out there erases everything in seconds." He shifted to a more comfortable position in the desk chair. "Guess we'll have to wait till your crime scene people finally make it here."

"You might do a little more in the way of investigation." Everard's voice was still sharp.

"I've got people to do that," Clements replied blandly. "They're getting prints and information from everybody else in the inn while you occupy yourself with Liza here." Ted Everard finally simmered down, and Liza finally got to bed—in a smaller room in the inn proper.

A knock on the door roused her. Belting her trusty bathrobe tightly closed, Liza went to answer. She blinked to find Sheriff Clements in the hallway—then blinked again. The electric lights were back on!

Clements nodded as he followed her gaze. "Yep, the juice is back, which means the computers are getting back up, too. Thought you'd like to know what we found out so far. A guest from California—a V. Tanner—paid for a night's lodging with a credit card that isn't exactly his. The card was from a company called Nostro Enterprises—even a hick cop like me knows it's a front company for organized crime."

The sheriff looked even more affable. "The prints came back under a different name. Turns out V. Tanner is actually one Vincent Tanino, aka 'Vinnie Tanlines'—a known associate of Fat Frankie Basso."

PART TWO:
Hidden Singles

This is another basic technique picked up almost intuitively by newcomers to Sudoku Nation. It rests on the rule that each nine-space subgrid in a puzzle can only hold one example of the magic numbers 1–9. Thus, discovering 1s in the subgrids located horizontally or vertically from a given box can prohibit a 1 from being placed in the three-space columns or rows within that box. Depending on where these forbidden zones fall around existing clues, a solver may find that there's only one available space that will take a 1. That number may stand hidden among a bunch of other candidates, but the logic is inescapable—there's only one true answer for that space.

I check for hidden singles first thing when I pick up a puzzle. And if I don't find any, I'll suspect this is a sudoku that requires heavy-duty solving techniques.

—Excerpt from *Sudo-cues* by Liza K

6

Liza decided on a room-service breakfast. For one thing, she didn't have the wardrobe to eat in the dining room. For another, she didn't want to try eating while looking at that damned annoying Ted Everard's face.

On the other hand, looking at my face might give him *indigestion,* she thought. Then she brushed the idea away. Considering the way he kept sneaking behind her last night, his area of personal interest lay in a whole other quadrant.

She rose at the knock on her door, tightening her robe yet again. Kevin stood in the corridor outside, a room service cart beside him. "I thought maybe we could have breakfast together up here."

"Why, no," Liza huffed, "I had my heart set on doing a Lady Godiva in your dining room."

Seeing Kevin's appalled expression, she switched gears, softening her humor. "Actually, you read my mind. In fact, you did better. I didn't want to go down there, but I didn't want to eat all alone, either." Liza grabbed his arm, pulling Kevin and the cart into her room. "Let's see how well you did at reading my mind and the menu."

"Actually," Kevin confessed as he set up a little table, "our regular morning cook didn't make it out here today. But Steve the bartender is pretty handy around a stove—and I helped." He took the cover off one plate. "Fried eggs, sunny-side up, with the yolks still runny enough to dip toast in them."

"Just the way I like 'em," Liza admitted.

Next Kevin uncovered a small tray. "Whole wheat toast for dipping—or if you prefer, English muffins."

"Mphmhm." Liza had already snagged half a slice and taken a bite.

Kevin continued, removing the cover from yet another plate. "Bacon, and Rocco's special sage sausage."

"How are we going to end this—with blood pressure and cholesterol pills?" Liza quipped. But she also took a deep appreciative breath, savoring the fresh-cooked scents.

"Oooh!" That breath came out as Kevin unveiled another platter with a smile. "Buckwheat cakes." Then he produced a small pitcher of purplish liquid. "With Rocco's personal blueberry syrup."

"Excellent!" Liza seized a knife and fork and began serving herself. "What are you having?"

"I—uh—thought we'd share." Kevin's voice sounded a bit plaintive as he watched her load her plate.

Liza frowned in thought. "Well . . . I did have a pretty good dinner last night, so I guess that's okay—just this once."

Grinning, Kevin tucked in as well. For a little bit, they ate in companionable silence. Finally, though, Kevin put down his fork with a sigh. "I know we said we'd never talk about last night—"

Liza shrugged. "Yeah, well, maybe I should have worn more going to bed. But then, I didn't expect a fire drill." She colored. "Or show-and-tell."

"I just wanted to say—" Kevin cleared his throat uncomfortably. "I'm sorry."

"I don't see why you should apologize," Liza said. "It's not your fault that Chris Dalen showed up here, or that

Fritz Tarleton made an appearance—or that it snowed like hell and I had to stay overnight." She gave him a rueful smile. "There's still plenty of winter ahead. With luck, we might have a romantic snowbound weekend sometime."

Kevin's eyes skittered around until he looked down at the table. "I just meant that I was sorry that you had to find another body. You're turning out like that old TV show about the rich couple that traveled around the world. Wherever they went, their friends either wound up dead or in jail."

"Oh, you mean *Hart to Hart*?" Liza chuckled. "Well, Chris Dalen was no friend of mine—even if he was an up-front, honest crook. And so far, the only one who looks likely to end up in jail is me, if Detective Ted Broom-Up-His-Butt Everard of the state police CID has his way."

"I don't think Bert Clements will go along with that," Kevin said. "He had his deputies take Vincent Tanino to the jail in Killamook for questioning as soon as the roads were cleared. And they brought Howard Frost to County Hospital after they got him a bit thawed out."

"Two less guests for you to worry about," Liza said.

"The state police forensics team arrived just after that, so they more than made up our head count." Kevin's eyes started roaming around the room again. "The cabin is still a crime scene—"

"And my clothes are part of the evidence," Liza said heavily.

"Um, yes," Kevin finally agreed. "So I've been poking around for some stuff that you could wear home."

"So what have you got, a maid's uniform? Painter's overalls?"

He looked up, a little shamefaced. "We have some clothes that wound up in lost and found—" Kevin held up his hands at her expression. "At least they're clean. We ran them through the laundry."

Do not bite his head off, Liza reminded herself. *He's trying to help you.*

She finally spoke up. "I've got another expansion idea for you—call it The Shops at Killamook Inn. We need a lingerie store, maybe a nice sportswear boutique—men's and women's . . ."

Kevin laughed. Then he stopped, a faraway look in his eyes. "You know," he said, "that's not such a bad idea, when you think about it . . ."

Liza sat uncomfortably in the passenger seat of Kevin's SUV, pulling the yellow slicker around herself. *I leave my house in my nicest outfit,* she fumed silently. *And I come home—well, look at me.*

Kevin had turned up another pair of galoshes, and she was wearing four pairs of socks to bulk up her feet so the damned things would fit. She had a pair of sweatpants that were too big, and a mismatched sweatshirt that was too small. As for lingerie, she was wearing a pair of boy's Jockey shorts that felt kind of peculiar.

When they turned onto Hackleberry Avenue, she gave a sigh of relief. Soon she'd be home, free to take another shower and get into her own clothes . . . They crunched their way through the snowdrift blocking the end of Liza's driveway, and Liza suddenly yelled, "Stop!"

Kevin braked heavily, jolting them to a halt. "What's the matter?"

"I just saw Mrs. H. at her door. She had a shovel." Liza pointed to her next-door neighbor's house, where Mrs. Halvorsen was already starting work on the pathway to the sidewalk.

"Kevin," Liza said, "she's not a young woman."

"We're not exactly kids ourselves," Kevin told her. "And from the way you were talking the other day, I bet she probably can't even afford the ten dollars she used to give me for the job when I was seventeen." Still, he sighed, went to the back of his big behemoth, and dug out a shovel.

Liza followed him, moving more clumsily in her improvised footwear. "Mrs. H.!" she called. "Let us give you a hand with that! Are you okay?"

"Oh, we had no trouble around here. We had electricity and everything." The older woman glanced at Kevin and then at Liza's outfit. "I hear that power was off at the inn."

"A lot of things were off at the inn," Liza told her.

"I was just going to dig my way over to see how Rusty was doing," Mrs. H. said.

"Oh, that would be far too much," Liza replied. They were already at the sidewalk now, and Kevin had begun to wield his shovel.

"Speaking of too much," he muttered, "do you know how many middle-aged men die of heart attacks from shoveling snow?"

"You're not middle-aged," Liza told him.

"I guess that will have to sustain me," he puffed as he worked. "Of course, if I'd known I'd be doing this, I might not have had eggs, bacon, and sausage for breakfast."

Liza made her way across the virgin snow to Mrs. H. Taking the woman's shovel, she set to work, soon meeting Kevin halfway. Then they started scraping their way over to Liza's house.

Rusty reacted to their arrival in much the same way that settlers in circled wagons greeted the cavalry riding in during an Indian attack. Happy barks echoed around the house, and his circles turned into arabesques when he saw Kevin and Mrs. H.—two of his favorite humans.

Checking in the kitchen, Liza saw that the dog hadn't gorged himself on the supplies she'd left, had done his business on the newspapers, and that a red-furred shadow had appeared beside her, expectantly looking up at the jar of doggie treats. "Here you go, you fraud." Liza opened the jar and gave him a treat.

"Really, you spoil that dog, dear," Mrs. H. reproved as

she sneaked another treat to Rusty. He circled both of them and then went to Kevin, hoping for a trifecta.

"Hey, guy, I bet you need to go out, don't you?"

Kevin's words momentarily erased the thought of treats from Rusty's mind. Rusty practically danced to the door while Kevin got his leash.

Mrs. H. stepped closer to Liza. "I heard there was more trouble at the inn than a power failure last night," she said. Her usually cheerful, round face looked strained, even nervous as she spoke.

"I don't know if it's something you'd like to hear about, Mrs. H." Liza shook her head. "It started as a pleasant evening, but it came to a bad end." Before she got any farther, the telephone rang. Liza sighed. She'd already noticed the insistent beeping from her answering machine. Excusing herself, she picked up the phone. Mrs. H. went to join Kevin and Rusty in the snow outside.

"Don't you ever turn on your damn cell phone?" Ava Barnes demanded. "I've been trying to get you since we had news about what happened at the Killamook Inn."

"The local cell tower was out, so there didn't seem much use in wasting my battery."

"But you are the one who found this art thief—Dalen?" Ava plowed on. "And there's a missing million-dollar painting? Is that why he was killed? Have you got any theories yet?"

"It's a Mondrian worth three million dollars," Liza replied. "If you heard anything about how the body was found—and what happened next—you'd know it's pretty embarrassing for me. And why should I have any theories about anything?"

"What?" Ava's voice got a little louder over the line. "You're going to solve this, aren't you? You solved the Derrick Robbins case down in Santa Barbara. I was there, remember? I almost got killed along with you. And you solved the mess that cropped up around the movie shoot here in Maiden's Bay. I figured you'd already be at work, out there with Sheriff Clements."

"For one thing, it's not just Sheriff Clements. There's an investigator from the state police who definitely doesn't want me butting in. For another, I don't want to get involved."

"How can you say that?" Ava's voice took on a "that's just crazy talk" tone—the tone of a managing editor seeing hopes for additional circulation flying out the window.

"As I remember it, you weren't all that eager to see me get involved in those other cases."

"Liza." Now Ava sounded like a schoolteacher trying to point out to an extremely dense student that two and two actually equal four. "Your column goes national in a couple of weeks. Think what it would mean if you also made the news pages in all those papers."

"Listen to me, Ava," Liza said. "I'm not getting involved in this. I mean it."

Well, they had literally been best friends for forever, painting sample polish on each other's bitten nails as kids, giggling over boys. Ava could tell when she was serious. Her brief silence showed that she'd gotten the message.

"We can talk about that later," Ava offered diplomatically. Then her managing editor side came out. "But there's still the story about what happened at the inn. You don't have to write anything," she said quickly. "I'll just put Murph on the line, and you can answer a few questions—"

"No," Liza said. "Give me a little time to get my head together, and then I'll come in. You'll understand a little better about how I feel after I talk with you."

Like how I'd hate to see all the juicy details splashed across the media, she added silently.

"Okay," Ava said uncertainly. "Later, then." She took a breath. "Which I hope means sooner, if you know what I mean."

"I know the paper has a deadline. Just give me a little time to sort things out. Bye, Ava." Liza hung up the phone.

Her fingers were still on the handset when the damned thing began ringing again. Had Ava thought up some new, last-minute argument? Taking a deep breath, Liza brought the instrument to her ear.

"I'd begun to think you had died instead of that art thief," Michelle Markson's voice came crisply across the line.

Michelle was not one to go gently into the night—or anywhere else, for that matter. She had used a forceful personality to create an impressive public relations fiefdom, her sharp tongue turning Hollywood movers and shakers into quakers instead. And even though Liza had attained the position of Michelle's partner, that didn't mean Michelle considered Liza her equal.

Michelle had her own plans for using the murder at the inn for publicity purposes. While her strategy resembled Ava's, her tactics were quite different.

"First and foremost, don't let your little friend on the *Podunk Gazette* think she's going to control the flow of information."

"It's the *Oregon Daily*," Liza corrected her for the fiftieth time.

"Whatever." Michelle didn't bother to keep the dismissive tone out of her voice. If a media outlet didn't have national penetration, she wasn't interested. The only local newspaper she paid any attention to was the *Hollywood Reporter*.

"Art theft is usually a bit too cerebral for the *Evening Entertainment News*," Michelle went on, mentioning one of the bigger TV tabloid shows. "They'll probably have to coach their people on how to pronounce Mondrian's name, but three million dollars should be understandable enough. The question is, how quickly can you uncover the murderer and find the picture? There's been a drought of good celebrity scandal—I swear to God, they were reduced to doing a piece on Shilon expecting her first permanent teeth last night."

"I'm not sticking my nose in this killing," Liza said firmly.

"You know, dear, you've achieved a certain reputation for figuring out what the police can't," Michelle pointed out. *A reputation that you've pushed pretty shamelessly while beating the drums for my new column,* Liza thought. "People might find it strange that you refuse to get into this case."

"I had strong reasons to get involved in those other cases," Liza said. "First a friend was murdered, and then a client had her career and film debut threatened. This time around, I don't have that kind of personal connection, and I'd prefer to let the professionals do it."

"I don't think this will help your reputation, Liza."

"But now you think playing detective will?" Liza glared at the phone. "Someone gave me an interesting sidelight on amateur sleuths—they either turn out to be cranks or publicity seekers."

"You make that sound like a bad thing," Michelle said sweetly. "Well, I wasn't expecting instant progress, anyway."

"Don't hold your breath," Liza warned. She hung up just as Rusty, Kevin, and Mrs. H. came back in.

"Well, that's gotten most of the silliness out of his system." Mrs. H. leaned down to scratch Rusty behind the ears.

"Oh, good. I thought you meant me." Kevin glanced at his watch. "But I'm afraid there's lots of silliness waiting for me back at the inn." Liza gave him the slicker and quickly changed into her usual parka to see Kevin out to his SUV.

As he drove away, Mrs. H. took hold of Liza's sleeve. "Could you come and join me for a cup of tea?" she asked. "I need to speak with you."

They were walking along the newly cleared path when they saw the first signs of traffic along Hackleberry Avenue other than Kevin's black behemoth. A nondescript sedan that might as well have been flying a flag that said "rental car" tried to get round Kevin—not an easy job given the size of his SUV and the width of plowed roadway. The car's rear wheels whined in slush and the vehicle fishtailed its way past, coming down the avenue toward them.

It pulled up in front of Mrs. H.'s house just as she and Liza arrived. The driver levered himself out and scrambled across a pile of shoveled snow to get to them. Liza recognized the brown polyester parka before she placed the pinched features. It was Howard Frost.

"Elise Halvorsen," he said, panting slightly as he came forward. "I'm with the Western Assurance Group—"

That was as far as he got. "Get off my property!" Mrs. H. shouted. "You're no better than a pack of thieves. And when I think of what you put us—me—through . . ." She stomped up the cleared path to her door, yanked it open, and then slammed it shut behind her.

That left Liza staring at the obnoxious insurance guy. He looked about as astonished as she felt. "I thought you were in the hospital," Liza said.

"I signed myself out," Frost told her.

Liza blinked. "And then you came all the way out here to annoy my neighbor? I thought you were after Chris Dalen. Is this just a side trip to see how well your company screwed Mrs. Halvorsen on her home repairs?"

Now Frost looked even more surprised. "Don't you know? Her married name is Halvorsen. But before that, your neighbor was Elise Dalen. She's Christopher Dalen's sister."

7

"Chris Dalen is dead," Liza said. "Why do you have to harass—"

"That doesn't end my business," Howard Frost interrupted. "There is still the matter of the missing painting, which my company is responsible for recovering." He paused for a second, adding, "Western Assurance Group has announced a ten percent reward for finding the Mondrian, so long as this does not involve guilty knowledge."

Liza looked over at the closed door. "Well, if Mrs. H. has any knowledge, I don't think she's in a mood to share with you right now."

Frost opened his parka and dug out a business card. "I'm staying at the Maiden Motor Court. If you happen to uncover any information—which I'm told you sometimes do—feel free to contact me."

Once again, Liza found herself saying, "Don't hold your breath."

While Frost made his way to his car, she headed up the shoveled walkway and knocked at the door. "It's Liza," she called, turning round to see the rental sedan pull away. "And nobody else."

The door opened, and Mrs. H. stood there, tears in her eyes. Liza grabbed the older woman's hands. "I didn't know—I'm so sorry—"

"It's not something I much wanted to talk about," she admitted, "having a convict in the family."

Mrs. H. took a deep breath. "He's my kid brother, the youngest of our family. When he was growing up, he always threatened to run away and join the circus. Maybe he should have. He had talent, he could have been a gymnast or the man on the flying trapeze, instead of spending all those years behind bars."

"If he talked about running away, I guess he mustn't have been all that happy at home," Liza said.

"We lived on a farm, and Chris hated it. As he got older, he used to give my father a hard time. Dad liked to say that he was his own boss, but Chris always needled him about really working for the bank." Mrs. H. looked down. "And he had a point. A couple of bad years, and Dad had some serious notes to pay off."

She shook her head. "My oldest brother inherited the farm. His kids sold the place to a larger operation, which got taken over by one of the big agribusinesses. They knocked down the house where we lived to put in a feedlot or some such. That was years after Chris left—or was taken."

"As in arrested?" Liza asked.

"Chris was always kind of a wild kid. Suddenly he had a lot of spending money. When my parents asked about it, he said he'd been doing some odd jobs. We found out just how odd when he got caught with a carload of computers he'd stolen out of an office building."

She shrugged. "My father refused to give him any help, and Chris wound up going to prison. Dad thought he'd learn a lesson. What he learned is that electronic stuff quickly loses its value, but art doesn't—and it's usually easier to carry. There were people who taught him the techniques, who helped set up jobs and sell off the proceeds."

"I guess your folks weren't so happy about that."

"They never spoke to him again, even when he turned up with lots of money in his pockets." Mrs. H.'s eyes began to tear up again. "No one was supposed to talk about him. When I got married, my husband Albert—well, he was a good man, but he was glad when his company transferred him down this way. No one knew the Dalens and what he used to call my 'scapegrace brother.' If I got the occasional letter from Chris, I always had to hide it. It would make Albert anxious—and angry."

She gave Liza a wry smile. "I thought Albert would have a fit when Chris got caught after this big job and wound up in Seacoast Correctional. Of course, he forbade me to go there." Mrs. H. shrugged. "But after he passed away, I would go and see Chris."

"It must have been very difficult for you," Liza said. "Like leading a double life."

"Not really," Mrs. H. admitted. "For a long time, it looked as if he'd never get out. Whenever Chris went up for parole, that awful man from the insurance company was there, arguing against it. He never missed a chance, like it was his religion or something." She looked bitter. "Usually, art thieves don't serve their entire sentences. Deals get made. All it takes is giving up the stolen picture."

Now it was Liza's turn for a wry smile. "But your brother had a stubborn streak. I saw that in our sudoku class."

"Chris said he'd rather die than let those phonies have it." Mrs. Halvorsen's lips trembled. "Now it looks as if that came true. It's not as if he had all that long to go. When he got sick, the doctors at the prison did their best, but—"

"He was going to stay with you," Liza said gently, remembering Dalen's words after he gave up his German shtick. "He told me at the inn. He was going to find a little job somewhere."

"I had told him about all the problems, how much it cost to fix the house. He said he'd do his best to help out." The older woman looked at Liza, her eyes bright with unshed tears. "Where else was he going to go? We were the last of our generation."

It took Mrs. H. a moment, but she got control of herself. "That reminds me of something I have to do as next of kin. Doc Conyers called—he's serving as the county coroner and needs a formal identification. That's why I had gotten to work with the shovel. And then when you came home, I wanted to ask if you'd come with me. But I didn't want to ask in front of Kevin."

"I understand," Liza said, "and I'd be glad to help." She gestured at her mismatched clothes. "Just let me change first."

Mrs. Halvorsen's eyebrows rose. "I was going to ask about those, too, but I didn't think I'd get an answer."

"It's kind of complicated to explain," Liza began, then shook her head. "So let's go with the short answer—you're right, you won't get one."

Back in her own clothes again, Liza helped Mrs. H. free her ancient Oldsmobile from the snow. Then they headed off for downtown Maiden's Bay. The parking situation looked pretty iffy, but they lucked out, finding a recently vacated spot not too far from City Hall.

The morgue was in the basement, in the opposite side of the building from the sheriff's department holding cells. Doc Conyers met them at the entrance. He was the town's general practitioner as well as the local coroner, an oversized sort of man with oversized facial features. As a kid, Liza had thought of him as very wise and very kind. As a grown-up, she suspected that Conyers would be a very difficult man to play poker against. Even so, she couldn't repress the feeling of trust that sprang up when she saw him.

"Elise, I'm sorry I have to ask this of you," Doc Conyers said. "And, Liza, thanks so much for coming along."

"Does this have to be done by the next of kin?" Liza found herself asking. "I mean, I taught a class at the prison. Chris Dalen was one of my students. If it's all the same, I could—"

Mrs. Halvorsen drew herself up to her full height, which brought her up to about Liza's shoulder. "I suppose I should appreciate your offer, but this is something I have to do." The insistent tone in her voice brooked no argument, so Liza didn't offer one.

"Come this way," Doc Conyers said. The doctor was wearing his usual baggy suit with a pipe sticking out of the breast pocket like some sort of sooty periscope. He offered Mrs. H. his arm as he led the way into a chilly tiled room that smelled of antiseptic. Directly ahead of them stood one of those floor-to-ceiling curtains you usually see in hospital rooms, except this one seemed heavier, as if it were backed with rubber . . .

Ewwww, I don't think I'm going to like this, she thought.

"They don't go for much in the way of amenities," Doc Conyers apologized. He pulled the curtain over to reveal what looked like an operating room.

No, Liza realized, this wasn't what she saw on the doctor shows. This was more like crime-scene TV. It was an autopsy room. A row of four small doors lined the far wall. They were all closed, but a hospital gurney stood in front of the last one. A sheet obscured the fact that someone lay on the stretcher.

Doc Conyers led Mrs. H. toward the gurney with slow steps. "I think you should get on her other side," he told Liza. Without thinking, Liza took the older woman's arm. The doctor stepped round, took hold of the top of the sheet, and gently brought it down so that only the face was exposed.

At least they had closed those horrible, staring eyes.

Mrs. Halvorsen began crying again. "That's my brother," she said.

"Yes, it's Chris Dalen." Liza was surprised to find her own voice choking up. Liza suspected this was not a part of the job Doc Conyers enjoyed. He led them away from the body with a flow of medical jargon that would have sounded like nervous babbling from a young intern.

"We'll need to do a complete postmortem. But on initial examination, it appears Mr. Dalen was attacked and subsequently strangled. That might be the cause of death, but it's possible that the stress brought on a fatal myocardial infarction."

"So it could have been another heart attack?" Mrs. H. asked faintly. "He wasn't—"

"I'm afraid it's murder, dear," Doc Conyers sounded grimly serious now. "Whatever killed your brother, someone else made it happen."

Doc Conyers had a couple of forms for Mrs. H. to sign, and then they were out of there. Liza might have considered it the bum's rush, except she was glad to leave the creepy environs of the morgue.

They drove most of the way back to Hackleberry Avenue in silence, until Mrs. Halvorsen finally said, "Chris was charming, even amusing. But he was a criminal. He told me that years ago, when he first wound up in prison, he had to fight and nearly got killed. I shouldn't take it as such a big surprise."

"He was an honest crook, Mrs. H." Liza found herself repeating her dinner conversation with Kevin. "Everyone in my class had good reason to be in Seacoast Correctional. But Chris was the only one to face up to that and admit it. And he was your brother."

Did that change things? Liza didn't want to think about it. Knowing Ava and Michelle, both of them would keep pushing her to look into the case. They'd both provide what information they could.

Guess it wouldn't kill me to use that, Liza thought as they arrived back at Mrs. H's house.

"I don't suppose you'd like to come in for a cup of tea, would you?" Mrs. Halvorsen asked.

Liza suspected her neighbor was more in need of company than refreshment. "Be glad to," she said.

They lurched over the plow-created snowbank at the end of the driveway, got out of the car, and walked along the shoveled path to the front door. "I was wondering," Liza said. "You said earlier that you'd gotten letters from your brother. Did you keep any of them?"

If Dalen had sent his sister a map with a prominent X or the address of a storage warehouse in Seattle, Mrs. H. would doubtless have mentioned it. But letters might give an idea of his movements and his associates.

Mrs. Halvorsen paused with her key in the lock. "I'd have to remember where I stuck them. Are you thinking of this as a case, dear?"

"I'm not sure," Liza admitted, "but I feel it would be worth a look."

Mrs. H. took off her coat, then rubbed her arms. "It's just about as chilly inside here as out." She complained. "Do you feel a draft?"

It seemed to be coming from the living room—the area where the tree had invaded. The heavy, old-fashioned furniture had been pulled into the archway that served as an entrance to the space. Beyond that was an empty space with traces of construction. The smashed-in wall and window had been cleaned up and squared off, with heavy-duty plastic stretched across the opening to protect against the elements.

Now, however, cold air was puffing through a slit in the plastic. Liza stepped over to peek outside. Maybe something else had fallen during last night's storm.

Instead, she found a trail of footprints leading up, then going off again.

8

"It looks as if someone walked up here and cut the plastic," Liza reported.

"Do you think they came in?" Mrs. Halvorsen quickly took a look around. "Well, they didn't get the TV or the video machine."

They wouldn't—unless they had an interest in antiques. Liza kept that thought to herself as her neighbor bustled around. First she went to the kitchen, where she picked up an old shoe box and began fingering through envelopes marked FOOD, GAS, ELECTRICITY. "My monthly budget seems untouched." Then she peeked into a sugar jar up on the third shelf of a cabinet—it turned out to contain a roll of bills. "And my mad money."

A quick trip upstairs brought the report that Mrs. H.'s jewelry was intact, too.

"Maybe whoever it was had just cut the plastic as we arrived and got scared off," Mrs. Halvorsen suggested.

Liza frowned, going over the area by the slit. "There's a little puddle here, as if whoever it was either stomped off snow or slipped off boots."

A considerate vandal, she thought—that didn't make much sense. *Unless whoever it was didn't want us to know where he—or she—had been. Maybe I'm not the only one wondering if Mrs. H. wound up with a big X-marks-the-spot map.*

She turned to her neighbor. "I think maybe someone came in here looking around—searching. Does everything look as if it's where it's supposed to be?"

Mrs. H. looked embarrassed. "With all the mess going on, I haven't been as neat as usual." She gestured to a corner of the dining room table, piled high with junk mail coming in and old newspapers on the way out. "I couldn't tell if that had been moved around if I wanted to."

"Do you want to call the police?" Liza asked.

Mrs. Halvorsen shook her head. "As far as I can see, nothing was taken. And the sheriff has more important business—a murder to solve."

After using some duct tape to seal the cut as best she could, Liza returned to her house. Rusty raised his head companionably from his patch of sunlight, but he didn't see the need to make a big point of her return. "No treats likely," Liza put it more bluntly.

She shook her head. "No use putting it off," she muttered, ringing up Ava Barnes.

Her boss on the *Oregon Daily* kept reasonably calm as Liza described everything that had happened the previous evening—although a sound suspiciously like a giggle came over the line a couple of times.

"It's not funny," Liza fumed into the phone. "You're the one who's all, 'Let's get ink about the syndicated column.' What do you think this would do for my public image if it came out?"

"Well, it gave me a great idea for a new comic strip—'Nuda, Warrior Princess'—" Ava broke off at the gagging sounds Liza began to make. "Look, I think that even your friend Michelle would have to admit there's no way to spin the story you just told me. All you can do is get people interested in a different story, like you trying to find the killer and the lost painting."

"Very neat," Liza complimented, "although maybe a bit self-serving." She sighed. "There's another wrinkle in the case you should be hearing soon. Chris Dalen is Mrs. Halvorsen's brother."

"You're kidding!" Ava burst out. "I have to get Murph right over there—"

"Cool your pits," Liza told her friend. "Mrs. H. isn't in any shape to talk to your ace reporter. She just came home from identifying the body."

"Murph is the right one for the job," Ava insisted. "You may not think so from the way he treats you, but he's very nice and polite with little old ladies. He says they remind him of his mother."

"He always told me he was an orphan."

"Well, maybe they remind him of the mother he never had." Ava's voice got a bit more sly. "It sounds as if this case is striking a lot closer to home than you thought at first."

"Do you know that the insurance company has offered a reward for finding the painting?" Liza asked.

"We just got a press release on the subject," Ava said.

"It's just—Mrs. H. is really having money problems. If I could help out—"

She broke off, thinking, I'm probably not the only one looking. That cut in the plastic around Mrs. H.'s house while we were away, that can't be a coincidence. While Sheriff Clements brought in Vinnie Tanino for questioning, Fritz Tarleton was probably free as a bird. And who knows? Maybe there are other people getting involved.

"So have you changed your mind?" Ava asked.

Liza sighed. "Let's say I'm thinking about it, so I'll do a little looking around."

"I guess I'll be happy enough with that as a start." Ava went back to serious business mode. "I've got people beginning to stack up outside my office. Do we have any other items to discuss?"

"I think that's enough," Liza replied. Saying good-bye, she hung up.

Then the phone rang again.

Liza shook her head as she told Rusty, "Y'know, I'm getting kind of tired of this." But her annoyance evaporated when she picked up the handset and heard Mrs. Halvorsen's voice.

The older woman sounded upset again. "Oh, Liza, I think I'm really losing it. We were there at the morgue, and I never thought to ask when they'd release Chris for services or a burial. How am I supposed to make the arrangements? I tried to call Doc Conyers, and all I got was his answering service."

"Well, I don't know that I can do any better," Liza started. Then she had an idea. "But maybe I have someone I can call."

She got off the line with Mrs. H. and punched in the number of Sheriff Clements's cell phone. "Liza," he said genially enough. "I guess you're safely home now."

"Thank heavens," Liza replied. "When I got back here, I discovered that my next-door neighbor is Chris Dalen's sister."

The sheriff's voice got a bit more serious. "Elise Halvorsen?"

"We went to the morgue to make an identification, and Doc Conyers told us that there'd have to be an autopsy. But Mrs. H. has to make plans for Chris's funeral, and she doesn't know when you folks will be finished with her brother's body."

She heard a rumble of voices—Clements must have put his hand over the receiver while he spoke with someone. Then he came back on. "I bet you wouldn't be surprised to hear that you can't throw a rock in downtown Killamook without hitting some media person. That's why we're sort of hiding out in the City Hall here in Maiden's Bay. What say you come down?"

"There's an invitation I don't get every day," Liza said. "Will I be there as a guest or a suspect?"

The hand must have gone over the receiver while Clements passed that along. Even so, Liza could hear the laughter.

"As a guest—we promise," the sheriff said.

"Then how can I resist?" Liza exchanged good-byes with the sheriff, pulled on her coat, and got the snow shovel to clear a path to her car. Soon enough, she was back in downtown Maiden's Bay. Unfortunately, Liza didn't have Mrs. H.'s parking luck. She had to deal with several slushy blocks to get to City Hall.

The police had one wing of the building. The officer on duty at the front desk must have been told to expect Liza, because he waved her straight back to the sheriff's office. Actually, it was more of a spare room/interrogation space equipped with a desk.

Sheriff Clements had installed himself behind the desk. Detective Ted Everard sat in another chair. Liza noticed he had gotten rid of his off-green suit. In fact, the state police investigator looked lanky but pretty good in a sweater and a pair of jeans, with what looked like a brand-new pair of duck boots on his feet.

Everard rose to hold another chair for Liza, but Clements spoke up. "Not that one, Ted. It's reserved for suspects."

"Ah." Everard shook the chair back slightly. "One leg too short, to keep whoever's being questioned from getting too comfortable?"

The sheriff looked bland. "I don't think it's forbidden by the Geneva Convention."

Liza suspiciously rattled a different chair before she settled in it.

"So what do you think of Ted's new duds?" Clements asked. "He just picked them up today at the army-navy."

"I've been in three other counties this week, living out of my suitcase," Everard groused. "I was down to my last clean shirt and my last clean pair of underwear."

"That may verge on too much information," Liza told him, thinking that at least the state cop had an excuse for the way he was dressed last night.

"I've asked Ted to stay on and give us the benefit of his experience," the sheriff went on. "He was quite an investigator before he became a glorified accountant."

"Yeah, well." Everard's embarrassment quickly turned to sour humor. "Besides, the way things seem to be going around here, I'll be logging some more major crimes."

"That may be," Liza said uncomfortably. "My interest is to find out about the postmortem for Mrs. H."

Sheriff Clements sat up straight in his chair to shrug. "I wish I could be more specific. We're bringing in a medical examiner with a bit more experience on criminal cases. Doc Conyers groused about it, but I think he's really relieved."

The sheriff brought up his hands. "Thing is, the weather is delaying our guy from getting down here. He's not going to arrive till tomorrow now, and it will be at least a few days until the whole thing is finished. Please pass my apologies along to Mrs. Halvorsen. As I know more, I promise I'll call her."

Liza nodded. "Okay."

Looking at her serious expression, Clements tried to lighten the mood. "So, any theories about what happened at the inn—or where this expensive painting might be lurking?"

That didn't amuse Everard. "No matter what you say, Bert, I don't think any investigation should depend on the girl detective and her chums."

"Well, besides what Liza brought to the table last time, her chums turned up information that helped us make a case—stuff we'd have had a tough time getting hold of."

"Even so," Everard growled.

Liza leaned over to pick up a digest-sized magazine that had fallen to the floor. *"Brain-Teasing Sudoku!"* she said brightly, trying to change the subject. "So, sheriff, are you trying out the nation's new puzzle craze?"

Clements grinned at her. "No, ma'am, that belongs to Ted."

"All right," the state police investigator mumbled. "I didn't make the connection between Liza Kelly and Liza K. Are you happy?"

"Me?" Liza said lightly. "Think of how my publicist will feel when I tell her about this."

"Oh, that's bad," the sheriff told Everard. "I've met that woman. She might just decide it's necessary to kill you."

Everard's answer was interrupted by the duty officer's appearance by the door. "Uh, the food delivery came from Ma's Café. I paid for it from petty cash like you said."

"I'd call this official business," Clements said, taking the open cardboard box. He set it down on his desk and dug out a burger with the works and a double order of french fries.

Everard, Liza was surprised to note, had a salad with chicken and an iced tea.

"You're not going for one of Ma's trademark Artery Buster Burgers?" she asked.

"I had to give up a lot of that stuff when I found myself driving a desk," Everard said. "It's kind of nice to be out in the field."

"Yeah, but you CID guys get to hear a lot of interesting stuff that never gets down to us hick sheriffs," Clements said. "Like about Frankie Basso."

"I don't know if you keep up with the crime news," Everard said to Liza. "But if you do, you might know that most of the organized crime up in Portland is controlled by the Russian mob and various Asian criminal cartels. Frankie had the job of diverting some of the business to homegrown organizations."

"Like dose guys from New Jersey?" Liza tried to do a gangster accent.

"Actually Vinnie Tanino worked for the Jersey mob, in his incompetent way. They bounced him off to La-la Land, where they figured he could do less damage grifting around the big hotel pools."

"Hence the nickname Vinnie Tanlines," Liza said.

"When Frankie Basso started recruiting for some muscle to Americanize Portland's crime scene, he gets Vinnie Tanlines dumped on him."

"What did Tanino have to say about last night?" Liza asked.

"He admits he was supposed to trail Chris Dalen. But he claims he got to Seacoast Correctional too late—Dalen had already gone. So he was just having a drink in the Killamook Inn, trying to figure out his next move, when he spotted Dalen at the bar. With the snow, he figured they'd both be stuck there, so he took a room. He didn't see Dalen after the early evening."

"So that's his story?" Liza asked.

"So far we can't prove otherwise," Everard replied. "Just as we can't prove otherwise regarding your statement."

Liza opened her mouth to protest, but something else came out instead. "But it does show that Frankie Basso was interested in the Mondrian."

"You mentioned it wasn't the first stolen art piece he was interested in, Ted," Clements said.

Everard shrugged. "If we believe Fat Frankie. Supposedly he bankrolled a museum heist just to be able to say he'd done it. The feds actually have him on tape talking about it." His lips twisted in a sour smile. "Problem is, there's no hard evidence. The art never turned up, and all the suspects met violent ends."

"Just like Chris Dalen." Liza rose from her seat, not sure what she'd learned here—except that Ted Everard was a lot more pleasant to be around when he managed to relax. "Thanks for the visit. I really should get back to Mrs. H."

As soon as Liza's car pulled into her driveway, the door to Mrs. Halvorsen's house popped open. Once again Liza trekked along the cleared path. The neighbors had been shoveling, too, and now a ribbon of cleared pavement ran down the block.

Stepping into her neighbor's house, Liza presented the sheriff's explanations and apologies. "I made some phone calls," Mrs. H. said. "Now I'll just explain that we have to wait."

She led the way to the living room. "I've also been thinking of how to move forward."

"Uh," Liza said brilliantly as the older woman picked up her bulky family Bible. It had been a long day and a longer night. She wasn't sure how much biblical scholarship she could take right now.

Instead, Mrs. H. retrieved a few sheets of paper hidden among the leaves. "This is where I hid any letters from Chris—my husband would never look here."

Unfolding the letters, Mrs. Halvorsen spread them on the table. "You can see that he traveled a lot. He makes a lot of comments about the towns he passes through, but there's very little about the people he meets or any friends."

She held up one sheet. "Except for this one. Here's the part. 'Look Ellie—' that's what he used to call me, Ellie— 'if you need to get in touch with me, leave a message with Phil Patrick at Patrician Books in Portland. I check in with him every so often.' " Reading her dead brother's words left Mrs. H.'s face looking sadder and older.

Her real age, the thought popped into Liza's brain.

"Well, there's a place to start," Liza said aloud. She copied down the address, then headed home. Of course, the phone started ringing the moment Liza opened her door.

"You know, you could make yourself useful by dragging the receiver down and barking at that," Liza told Rusty as he went into his usual *woof*-and-circle dance. "Yeah?" she finally said when she got the damned thing to her ear.

"Not even snow can cool the temper of my lady love," the voice on the other end teased.

"What do you want, Michael?"

Michael Langley, who would soon be Liza's ex-husband if they ever got the last of the paperwork cleared away, sounded hurt. "I was calling to see how you were. After a not-very-informative conversation with your answering machine last night, I heard you'd gotten involved in another murder." His voice got a little flat. "At the Killamook Inn."

"Michael—"

She didn't get any further as Michael pressed on. "Anyway, I booked a flight to get up there, but the only airport I could get was Portland."

Liza sighed. When Michael got this tone, it was no good trying to persuade him otherwise. "I'll pick you up. When are you arriving?"

She wrote down Michael's flight information on the same piece of paper she'd just gotten from Mrs. H., said good-bye, and then started dialing Kevin's office at the Killamook Inn.

"Michael's flying up tomorrow morning," she said when Kevin picked up. Taking a cue from Michael, she plowed over Kevin's next words. "Now I can go in my own car, but I expect the roads will still be crappy, so it would be better to go in your SUV."

Then, before Kevin could raise a head of steam in his protests, she added, "And since we'll be in town, I'd like to check out a message drop Chris Dalen was known to use."

9

They weren't even out of the airport parking lot, and Kevin and Michael were already sniping at one another. Liza tried to keep her mouth shut, determined not to pour gasoline on the fire.

Morning had brought weather that was warmer, but pretty gray and cheerless—much like Kevin's mood as he picked her up. He was not happy about going to collect Michael. He was even less happy when Liza had mentioned the bookshop. But what really made him unhappy was reading about Mrs. Halvorsen's connection to Chris Dalen in the morning newspaper.

Murph the reporter must have worked his usual little-old-lady magic, because there were liberal quotes from her neighbor in the story, which featured a childhood sister-and-brother picture, a mug shot of Chris Dalen, and a recent shot of Mrs. H. at this year's garden festival.

The tone was pretty gentle—high-spirited farm boy became famous art thief when his biggest coup went wrong. Of course, the story also pointed out that Dalen had spent so much time behind bars because he wouldn't give up the

Mondrian he'd stolen. Mrs. H. was pretty forthright about that: "When I saw Chris's picture in the papers, he'd been out of my life for years. I had no idea what he'd been up to, and I never asked him about it."

Kevin, on the other hand, had a lot of questions about what Liza thought *she* was doing.

"I'm just trying to get Mrs. H. some answers about her brother," Liza said.

That didn't satisfy Kevin. "Strikes me the biggest question is, 'Where did that big-bucks painting end up?' That's probably the question that got Chris Dalen killed." He glanced from the empty road ahead to her for a moment. "And if you start asking questions about Dalen, whoever killed him is going to think that's the answer you're really after."

So neither of them was in a great frame of mind even before they got to PDX. And when Michael got in the backseat, he was carrying a lot more luggage than the duffel hanging from his shoulder.

"Funny, you didn't mention you were going off to the inn for dinner," Michael said after he got settled.

Yeah—real funny, Liza thought. But she thought better of actually saying it.

"Especially with that weather. You'd have to think there was a good chance of getting stranded out there."

Liza couldn't let that pass. "We moved up dinner, so I would have gotten home earlier if everything had worked out. Unfortunately, Kevin had business—"

"Yeah, I wonder what kind of business that was— considering what Curt Walters had to say about the way they found you." Kevin braked with more than necessary vehemence when some idiot cut them off. Michael went on as if nothing had happened. "Yeah, I got to be pretty friendly with Curt during my last stay up in Maiden's Bay. His comments made a sort of interesting sidelight to the media reports."

"Curt made a lot of—" Liza was going to say "stupid," but she changed that to "unhelpful comments during a pretty embarrassing situation."

"A situation you could have avoided if you'd kept your pants on," Michael's former mild tone started disintegrating. "Or if you'd decided not to stay the night."

"Funny," Kevin said, "how some people get so controlling when their divorce is just about to be finalized."

"Yeah? Well, it's an amicable divorce," Michael replied. "We've been really amicable lately. And things could just as easily go amicably the other way—if we were just left alone."

"'Left alone?'" Kevin echoed. "Isn't that why Liza came back to Maiden's Bay? Because she was left alone after you walked out on her? And then you come worming your way back in—"

"And you haven't been worming away yourself ever since I left for that script job?" Michael retorted. "As soon as my back is turned, you're trying to get her to play house in that overgrown pile of Lincoln Logs you manage—"

As the conversation grew hotter, Liza frantically fished around in the glove compartment for Kevin's map of Portland. "Let's see if we can track down the address for this bookstore where Chris Dalen used to get messages," she said, trying to sound like an adult. God knew, the other people in the car sounded like teenage boys.

Sensing Kevin's resistance, Michael enthusiastically embraced the idea. But then, he'd just as enthusiastically have opened the door to play in traffic if Kevin had said that was dangerous.

"What do you think you're going to find?" Kevin demanded. "An envelope with big handwriting—'For my dear sister in the event of my death'? If there was anything that might point the way to the painting, we'll probably find the store closed and the owner off trying to dig up the Mondrian. There's no honor among thieves."

"Maybe—maybe not," Michael replied. "We can't know what we might find out until we check the place—and the owner—out." Liza rolled her eyes. At least she'd gotten them fighting over a different topic.

Patrician Books didn't look particularly patrician. The shop was a dingy storefront in a neighborhood that had managed to avoid Portland's rising tide of prosperity. The grand name was emblazoned on a wooden sign whose hand painting was flaking away.

Phil Patrick didn't live up to his name, either. Liza had envisioned a small tough guy, like the sort of characters Jimmy Cagney played in those old black-and-white gangster films on the classic movie channels. An ex-bantamweight boxer, maybe.

The real-life Phil Patrick wasn't so much a bantam as a big chicken. Liza knew chickens. One of her grammar school classmates, Suzy Dorling, had lived on the outskirts of town—where all the Californians were erecting their McMansions these days. Back then the area was considerably more rural, and Suzy's parents had raised chickens. Liza had gotten to see the dynamics of a flock, including the pecking order. There was always one scruffy-looking chicken that all the rest could pick on—or peck on.

Phil Patrick was the human equivalent.

They had first spotted him while they were parking. Patrick was still setting up for business, struggling to push a decrepit wooden bin full of tattered paperbacks. He chained it to the gate in front of his store. The heavy steel barrier was only pushed far enough to open the door.

By the time Liza, Kevin, and Michael crossed the street, Patrick was back inside the store. He was a tall, skinny type, a little too tall for the sagging jeans he wore. He had some sort of rash that left the exposed skin on his hands and face blotchy, cracked, and red. His quick nervous mannerisms only increased his chicken resemblance. Even his moth-eaten, out-at-the-elbows sweater looked like bedraggled plumage.

"What can I do for you folks?" He stood rubbing some sort of salve into his hands with quick, obsessive gestures, his head jittering and his eyes darting around as he addressed them. Liza wondered if he'd had to deal with so many customers at once lately.

"We understand you picked up messages for Chris Dalen," Kevin began.

Patrick's head began bobbing faster, as if he were a chicken working up the nerve to try taking a peck at them. "I dunno why people are digging that up," he complained. "Some guy was on the phone right when I opened up, tryna put the screws to me, sayin' how bad things were gonna get if I didn't tell him everything I knew about that damned Mondrian."

His voice came out as a whine, and his lower lip hung down to reveal snaggled, stained teeth. "That's something that's been over and done with for years. Sometimes people would call or drop a message for Chris—whether it was about jobs or what, I didn't ask. Then, every week or so, Chris would call in. He'd buy a book or throw me a few bucks. But I ain't seen him since before his big score. That would have to be nearly fifteen years, now."

Liza wasn't sure Patrick was as legitimate as he claimed to be. Standing in this dark, cluttered space, breathing in the smells of decaying wood and crumbling paper—with a whiff of unwashed Phil Patrick on the side—she figured the man needed something more than book sales to pay the rent on this place.

On the other hand, she couldn't imagine Dalen using this pathetic character as anything but a go-between.

"So you never had anything to do with the Mondrian?" she asked.

"Nothin'—except for hangin' it up on the wall here."

"What?!" Kevin and Michael's hopes of finding the stolen painting on the humble wall of the shop crashed pretty quickly.

Oh, it had the juxtaposed squared-off blocks of color

usually associated with the Mondrian style. But it was just as obvious that this Mondrian was a page-sized photo cut from a magazine. Even in the dim light of the bookstore, it had faded against the varnished wood of the wall.

"There it is," Phil Patrick said, *"Composition in Blue, Red, and Green."*

"That," Kevin burst out, "is worth three million bucks?"

Patrick shrugged. "Mondrians don't come cheap. And this one was kinda special. That Mondrian guy wasn't real fond of the color green—he didn't use it much. So this thing was worth another coupla bagfuls of money from the dot-communist who bought it and was showin' it off at the museum."

Like a kid with a rare baseball card, Liza thought. She suddenly remembered Chris Dalen's comment on his big haul—how it looked like a schematic for a tiled bathroom floor.

"Course, it's bigger and probably better lookin' in real life," Patrick helpfully added.

I hope so, Liza thought as she and the guys left the store.

Detective disappointment kept both males in the SUV quiet all the way home to Maiden's Bay. No sooner did they pull into the driveway than Mrs. Halvorsen came hurrying over.

Well, I guess she could use the company, Liza thought.

"I don't even know why I'm here," Mrs. H. confessed when she came in the door. Kevin had taken Rusty outside, and Michael was upstairs taking the antihistamine that allowed him to be near the dog without sneezing his head off.

"I'm afraid we didn't learn very much," Liza said. "The man at the store wasn't really a friend of your brother's. He says he wasn't in touch with him even before Chris was arrested."

Coming back down the stairs, Michael tried to make a joke. "I'd say that guy wasn't the type to send cards out to anyone at Christmas, either." He came over and took Mrs. Halvorsen's hands. "Hi, Mrs. H. How are you holding up?"

"I've had better days," the older woman admitted. "I'm glad you came up."

"It was sort of a spur of the moment thing," Michael said. "I don't even have a place to stay. I don't suppose your spare room—?"

He broke off as the tears began to flow.

"Of all the insensitive—" Kevin, who had just reentered with Rusty, immediately started to fume. "Didn't you realize who was going to be in that room? Why she had you redo it?"

That's a pretty high horse he's gotten on, for somebody who didn't have a clue two days ago, Liza thought.

"I'm sorry." Michael looked appalled as he apologized. "I didn't think—"

"It's always about you, isn't it?" Kevin demanded. "Barging in on people, walking out on your wife." Michael looked about ready to haul off and punch Kevin, which was probably what Kevin was looking for. It would give him the chance to wipe the floor with Liza's semi-estranged husband.

Liza was almost ready to step in and say that Michael could stay with her. A disastrous move—that would really tick Kevin off. But Mrs. H. stepped between the two men, taking each by the arm.

"After Chris had his first heart attack, I hoped that he finally might get out of that place . . . that he might come home." Then she turned to Michael. "Of course you can stay."

As if to underscore the happy moment, the phone rang.

"I swear to God, I'm going to pull that wire out," Liza growled, picking up the handset.

"Liza, dear." Michelle's voice came over the line as a smooth purr. "I just had a brief chat with your friend Ava. She tells me you're looking into this matter after all. Does that make you a crank or a publicity hound?"

"It makes me the friend of a neighbor who's having trouble." Liza glanced around at the other people in the room. "In fact, Mrs. H. is right here with me, along with Kevin and Michael."

"Excellent!" Michelle said. "Put on the speakerphone. I've got Buck Foreman tied in, too, for some professional input."

Buck Foreman was the investigator of choice for Markson Associates. He'd had a good career as a cop destroyed by bad publicity. Michelle had tried to help him, and that business bond had become personal. Buck's willingness to help out with Liza's sometimes fumbling investigations was proof of how strong that relationship was.

"Liza." Buck's voice came out as about one tone north of a growl. "Anything that's not already in the media? We've got all that."

"Did they talk about Vinnie Tanino? A guy who works for Fat Frankie Basso?" Liza asked.

Buck actually laughed. "Vinnie Tanlines is involved in this?"

"So, I think, is Fritz Tarleton, the big man in the tourism business. He was at the Killamook Inn, probably to negotiate for the Mondrian."

"Kevin?" Buck asked. "You think you could get us a list of the other people staying at your place?"

"Give me a minute." Kevin pulled out his cell phone. After a brief conversation with John the assistant manager, he began reciting the list. When he got to "R. Carlowe," Buck interrupted.

"Did you actually meet this guy? Built like a tank, face like a lizard?"

"I didn't have the pleasure." Kevin passed the description on, and then nodded. "John says that's an apt description."

"You know him?" Michelle rapped out.

"Yeah." Buck didn't sound as if the word made him happy. "He's what people call a Hollywood detective."

Michael laughed. "You're kidding!"

"What's so funny?" Kevin wanted to know.

"I thought that was a made-up thing. They used to have stories about Hollywood detectives in the old pulp magazines of the thirties—the off-color, spicy ones. They still had Hollywood detectives in the sixties, now in cheesy paperbacks. Gat in one hand, blonde in the other, beautiful starlets in negligees falling madly in bed with them."

"The reality isn't so interesting," Foreman said dryly. "Back in the thirties, the Hollywood studios had their own fixers to deal with embarrassing situations. More recently they've outsourced, using private investigators to look into wrongdoing or to get the goods on associates or to help make embarrassments go away—also known as witness tampering."

"You don't—" Kevin began.

"No, I don't," Buck finished for him. "But Rod Carlowe would. We used to be colleagues, once upon a time in L.A."

"He was a cop?" Michael said.

"A dirty one," Buck's voice was flat. "But he's done well in his niche, even become something of a celebrity. Knowing Rod, he's probably angling for a reality show. If he's involved . . ."

Buck's voice died away for a second. Then he abruptly asked, "Anything out of the ordinary happen around your neighborhood?"

"I had a vandal," Mrs. H. announced. "Part of my house is under construction and wrapped in plastic, and somebody made a cut in it."

"Did they?" Buck sounded extremely suspicious. "Liza," he said, "you can expect me tomorrow. I'll rent a car wherever I land and call you with an ETA."

"We don't seem to be getting very far," Michelle finally broke in. "But then I expect the Great Wall of China just started with a few rocks. I'll expect better results the next time we speak, Liza."

Liza didn't even get a chance to respond. The connection was cut.

A second later, Michael and Kevin were back in bickering mode, Kevin talking about Michael imposing himself, Michael casting himself as the protector of Casa Halvorsen. Liza found herself rubbing her temples.

"If you're going to move in, Michael, maybe you'd better get your duffel and move along with Mrs. H.," she finally said. "And Kevin, I don't remember your recitation of guests, but is Mr. Tarleton still at the inn?"

That got Kevin moving to his SUV, bringing Michael and Mrs. H. along. Liza cheerfully waved good-bye, moving to block the door so that Rusty couldn't get out.

She plopped herself in front of the computer, intending to get some work done. But she found she couldn't concentrate and only managed to work out one puzzle after messing up a couple of puzzles with rookie errors.

	3						8	
2			5		6			4
			2	7	8			
		9		6		8		
7			1		2			3
		3		5		7		
			7	9	3			
3			6		1			2
	6						3	

Finally she got up and went to the attaché case she'd
taken to her class, retrieving the puzzle Chris Dalen had
given her. Liza input it to her Solv-a-Doku program and
then looked at the result on the screen.

When she'd solved the murder of her friend Derrick
Robbins, Liza had wound up with a rather strange legacy—
Derrick's very specialized library on sudoku and cryptog-
raphy. That case had shown Liza how a message could be
encoded into a sudoku puzzle. And reading some of the
volumes on ciphers had only suggested more methods for
illicit communication.

She suddenly remembered how furious Howard Frost
had been at the idea that anything Chris Dalen had written
might leave the prison. Could there be some meaning buried
in this seventeen-clue wonder? Liza bit her lip, going over
the clues and then the finished puzzle. Could the grid hide a
substitution code where numbers replace letters? Well if it
did, it wasn't just a straight 123 for ABC swap.

Hmph. Chris Dalen's name didn't repeat any letters.
That could serve as the key for another type of cipher, with
the letters from the name first in line and the remaining letters lined up alphabetically behind it. Thus, $C=1$, $H=2$,
$R=3$, $I=5$, $S=6$, $D=7$, and so on.

Unfortunately, that system didn't yield a message, either. Oh, there were other number codes. Numbers could
be used to find a page in a book, a line on the page, and a
word in the line. Should Liza ask Mrs. H. if her brother had
some favorite reading matter?

*I think I'd be better off asking some questions of Uncle
Jim,* Liza thought. Jim Watanabe came from the Japanese
side of Liza's Hibernasian family tree. He worked for the
Foreign Service in Tokyo—and seemed to know a lot about
codes and secret messages for a State Department paper-
pusher. Though her uncle never spoke about it, Liza suspected he was some sort of spy. Throughout the Cold War
and after, Japan was a major listening post for Soviet and
Russian communications.

Going online, Liza clicked on the Instant Message icon.
Japan was eight time zones behind Pacific Standard Time,
but she noticed that Uncle Jim apparently kept an eccentric
schedule.

Hey, Uncle Jim, she typed and then stared at the un-
changing screen as seconds turned to minutes. Finally, Liza
ripped off a nasty word and closed the window on her computer. Obviously, Uncle Jim wasn't available to chat. Liza
began composing an e-mail.

Uncle Jim, she began, **Here I am asking for your help again.**
She explained the background and the methods she'd used,
then attached the puzzle and its solution.

Dunno if this will get us anywhere, Liza thought. *But
I've got to do something.*

•

10

Liza was awake when Buck Foreman called the next morning. At least her eyes were open, although she was lying in
bed with the pillow over her head.

Last night had not been easy. The Kelly Dreamland
Movie Show had been a more graphic remake of *Liza Dis-
covers Dalen*. This version had apparently been edited for
the teen multiplex market. Chris Dalen came bursting out
of the mattress the way Alien had exploded from that hapless guy's chest.

Liza had scrambled across a bed that seemed to stretch
to the horizon, pursued by Chris, his pale hands stretched
out to touch her. His eyes were still lifeless and staring, but
his lips were now set in that familiar crooked grin.

He whispered after her in that hokey German accent,
"Zere iss no ezcape . . ."

After three replays on the inside of her eyelids, Liza had
sat up in bed, deciding she could do without sleep for a few
hours. Then she'd finally fallen into a dreamless, exhausted
slumber.

Luckily, Buck had called from the airport car rental instead of a block away from Hackleberry Avenue. His trip to Maiden's Bay gave Liza a chance to shower and wash some of the stupor away. A cup of coffee and some slightly stale cereal (that was the only breakfast food in the house) completed the wake-up process.

She had let Rusty out to do his business, fed him, finished a second cup of coffee, and checked her e-mail by the time Buck arrived. He didn't have his usual sunglasses on in the gray weather, but he still looked every inch the hard-ass cop he once had been. As she opened the door for him, she noticed that Buck carried the kind of junior suitcase that salesmen use to tote around samples.

"How ya doin', Liza?" Buck asked, stepping into the house.

"Well, I'm awake."

A grin appeared on Buck's great stone face. "I don't know that anyone connected with Markson Associates was an early riser—except maybe Ysabel."

Ysabel Fuentes was the firm's receptionist. With her knowledge of the foolishness and foibles of Hollywood's A-list, she probably wielded more power than most studio line producers. She also regularly got into wars with Michelle, quit, and then came back to work after Liza conducted extensive shuttle diplomacy.

Buck's grin grew even more evil. "Ysabel stormed off around midafternoon yesterday. Michelle has gone through three temps so far."

With Michelle, there was always the possibility that Buck was speaking literally. Liza shot a worried glance at the bag he carried. "You're not bringing body parts up here to dispose, are you?"

Buck patted the case. "No, this is for the field trip we'll be taking to your friend's house. Is she the round-faced lady I saw peeking out from next door as I came up the driveway?"

Liza nodded. "The hatchet-faced biddy on the other side got into a fight with my mom about thirty years ago and hasn't spoken to a Kelly ever since."

"Well, since your Mrs. Halvorsen is home, let's go and pay her a visit."

The door to Mrs. H.'s house flew open even as they approached. Liza came in and gave her neighbor a hug, checking to see if the older woman was chilly. "How's the duct tape holding up on that slit?" she asked.

"Oh, fine. Michael put on another layer yesterday evening." Mrs. H. glanced over at Buck. "Aren't you going to introduce me to your friend?"

"Oh, no, ma'am," Buck said, "I'm just here to read the meters."

He opened his case to reveal a whole collection of high-tech gizmos, each carefully nestled in foam packing. Selecting one about the size of a pack of cigarettes, he turned it on, illuminating a small light on the top of the gizmo. It immediately began blinking. With a finger to his lips, Buck began walking around the living room. A beeping noise began to come from the little box in his hand. It grew faster as he approached the mass of displaced furniture pushed against one wall.

Buck dropped to one knee and produced a penlight, which he shone under an armchair. After a moment of fishing under the furniture, he came up with something about the size and shape of a telephone pager—except this thing had an aerial on top.

He brought it over the bare floor, dropped it, and then crushed the gizmo under his heel.

"What was that?" Liza asked. "Some kind of a bug?"

Buck nodded, still waving around his box—his bug finder, Liza now realized. She noticed that the light on the gizmo was off, now.

"I didn't think he'd have more than one in here. That was a radio transmitter," Buck announced, "a Rod Carlowe special. He loves his technotoys. About forty or fifty feet from here, there's probably a receiver plugged into a long-term recording device. I don't think Rod would bother doing a full-time live surveillance—begging your pardon, ma'am," he said to Mrs. H.

"None taken," Mrs. Halvorsen said faintly. She was having a hard time dealing with the fact that anyone would want to spy on her.

"Rod probably swings by his listening post and checks the recording each day," Buck went on. "He heard about that bookstore being used as a drop and called before Liza even got over there." Liza briefly explained that development from yesterday's visit to Portland.

"And this is why I have that big cut in the plastic over there?" Mrs. H. asked.

"Well, it was an easy enough way for Rod to get in here," Buck said. "He probably tossed—ah, did a brief search," he amended with a glance at the older woman.

"Liza suspected that much." Mrs. H. looked a little embarrassed. "Looking around, I couldn't be sure."

"Well, it would probably be enough to make people worry about that—rather than realizing he'd been bugging the place."

"You think there are more?" Liza asked.

Buck held up his little box. "Well, I've got a radio frequency detector here. Let's go and see." They found another of the little boxes established beside Mrs. H.'s phone, and a final one in the upstairs hallway. Michael emerged from his room as Buck destroyed that one.

"Is that what I think it was?" Michael asked incredulously.

"If you thought it was a listening device." Buck ranged the top of the house, but his detector remained lightless and quiet.

Michael was down on his hands and knees, examining the wreckage. "Kind of bigger than I expected," he said. "And is that a cell phone battery?"

"Yeah, the ones the size of a straight pin run by microscopic nuclear reactors pretty much only belong in spy movies," Buck said somewhat sarcastically. "I thought you were one of those writers who did your research."

"I never had to use one of these—in a story," Michael quickly added. He continued to poke at the debris. "Is this expensive?"

"You could probably get one in your friendly neighborhood spy store for about two bills or a little more," Buck said. "It's definitely not top-of-the-line, but it's enough for this job." He grinned a not particularly nice grin. "Rod probably buys them by the gross."

He led the way downstairs, saying, "Now that we know the place is clean, I have some information." He paused. "But I think you'd better ask your friend Kevin to join us. That way the whole team will be here."

Liza suddenly found herself remembering Ted Everard's comment about the girl detective and her chums. However, judging from the look in Buck's eye, she suspected this professional detective had plans of getting some information, too.

Kevin arrived, and they adjourned to the kitchen, where Mrs. H. was busily brewing tea. "Michelle and I both spent some time digging up information after we spoke to you yesterday," Buck began.

"Do you know who this Carlowe guy is working for, or is he here on his own?" Michael asked.

That got another grin from Buck. "Actually, he's working for an old friend of Liza's—Alvin Hunzinger."

"He's not exactly a friend," Liza protested.

"Nonsense." Buck smiled maliciously. "Think how he rushed to your side to free you from the clutches of the police down in Santa Barbara."

Liza blushed. Alvin Hunzinger looked like a cartoon character—in fact, he was a dead ringer for Elmer Fudd in the old "Looney Tunes." "He rushed there because he's scared to death of Michelle," she said tartly. "Which I guess anyone who makes his living as the lawyer to the stars should be."

"Which star is he working for?" Mrs. H. asked excitedly.

"A former child star—of the boardroom," Buck replied. "Conn Lezat."

Liza blinked. "Okay, Conn and Chris Dalen were both in my class. But I don't see any reason why Lezat would be involved with Chris."

"In the course of his career, Hunzinger has dealt in several cases of recovering stolen art," Buck explained. "It looks as if Lezat has him trying to turn up the stolen Mondrian to cut a deal."

"Well, it would improve Lezat's image as America's Most-Hated White-Collar Criminal." Liza could see the public relations advantages in that.

"And maybe he'd be able to get some years knocked off his prison term," Kevin finished.

"You had Carlowe on the list of people who were stranded at the inn when Dalen, uh—" She glanced at Mrs. Halvorsen.

"When my brother was murdered," Mrs. H. said unflinchingly.

Liza intertwined her fingers and then rested her chin on top of them. "Great," she groused. "That means we've got somebody representing Fat Frankie Basso, somebody representing Conn Lezat, and Ritz Tarleton's very own daddy at the Killamook Inn at the time of the crime."

"Sounds like a pretty full house," Michael said to Kevin.

Liza looked from one to the other of the men in her life. *Well,* she thought, *if they really start acting like idiots, Buck can slap them down—one at a time or both at once.*

"So," she said aloud, "I guess we have to apply the MOM test: motive, opportunity, and means. So, motive—they all have some reason for wanting the Mondrian."

"Three million dollars hanging on your wall, even if it's a wall in your vault—that could make somebody lose his head," Michael said.

"Or maybe as a very expensive get-out-of-jail card," Kevin put in.

"Opportunity," Liza pressed on. "Again, we've got a tie. Vinnie Tanino, Rod Carlowe, and Fritz Tarleton—"

"With entourage," Kevin added sourly.

"Were all at the Killamook Inn on the night Chris Dalen was murdered," Liza finished. "When you come to means, though, I think the needle starts to point to Vinnie Tanino. He's not a great criminal mind, I'll grant you, but he is a mobster. I don't think he'd hesitate to rough someone up to get information."

"And you think," Mrs. H. paused to take a deep breath. "You think he went too far?"

"He also tried to hide his identity with that dodgy credit card," Kevin said slowly.

"All valid points," Buck conceded. "But I wouldn't rule out any of the other guys. Remember, I knew Rod Carlowe when we were on the force together."

"The police," Michael said, seeing the puzzled expression on Mrs. Halvorsen's face.

"Rod wasn't above beating a confession out of a suspect if investigating looked like a lot of work. Sometimes he put innocent people away."

Buck shook his head. "After he got bounced out, he didn't develop a greater reverence for human life. A couple of years ago, a studio bigwig was fighting this court case. Carlowe tried to blackmail a witness for the other side into changing his testimony. Instead, the guy committed suicide. Saint Rod not only held up his client for a bonus, he went out and spent it on an all-night party."

"Sounds like a charming fellow," Liza said.

"And from what Michelle tells me, Fritz Tarleton wouldn't be fitted for a halo anytime soon," Buck went on. "When his daughter Ritz started out on the Hollywood scene, she hooked up with a lowlife lounge lizard. Papa no like. He had his head of security, Jim McShane, lay a beating on the unsuitable boyfriend to discourage him."

"You know," Liza said, "I'm beginning to see where Ritz gets her whole 'little people's rules don't apply to me' attitude."

Kevin looked frankly unhappy. "McShane—that's one of the people staying with Tarleton at the inn."

"Could this man have killed my brother?" Mrs. H. demanded bluntly.

"I don't know," Buck told her. "He's a former cop from New York City—that's where Tarleton has his headquarters. We're trying to get some kind of line on McShane's past."

"Any other tidbits?" Michael asked.

"Here's one," Buck said. "When he started getting into the big money, Tarleton got a reputation as an avid art collector—and not a good reputation."

"See?" Michael said. "He's one of those guys who'd sit in his vault and gloat over a painting only he can see."

Liza had a more practical question. "What gave him that reputation?"

"Some federal charges over paying bargain-basement prices for Mesopotamian antiquities that turned out to be looted from Iraqi museums," Buck replied.

He sat back in the chair where he'd settled himself, looking over his audience. "Michelle turned up a possible source of information, not on what happened to Chris Dalen, but about what he did with the Mondrian."

He turned to Mrs. Halvorsen. "When your brother got arrested, did you know the lawyer who represented him?"

"I didn't get to find out anything about the case," Mrs. H. confessed. "My husband would have burst a blood vessel if I'd tried. And since—" She shrugged. "Well, Chris and I never talked about it."

"Well, your brother went to trial with a Portland criminal attorney named Lewis Partland. There wasn't much Partland could do—he faced an open-and-shut case. In the years since the case, Partland retired . . . to a town called Otis."

"That's about forty miles from here, give or take," Liza said. "Just go down the 101—"

Buck nodded. "And that's what we're going to do."

"I—I can't," Kevin stammered. "I only took a quick break to come over here—"

"Yeah," Michael said sarcastically. "Hurry back to your precious inn. Protect your job." Liza put a hand on Buck's shoulder, ready to propel him into the middle of things when Kevin swung at Michael. Instead, Kevin flinched. Then, without a good-bye to anybody, he left.

"Ah, man," Michael said after the door closed. "I didn't mean—"

You didn't think, Liza thought, frowning. *And I didn't think Kevin was taking his situation so seriously.*

11

"I'm afraid I won't be going with you," Mrs. Halvorsen spoke up. She put her hands to her face. Liza reached out a hand to Mrs. H.'s shoulder. The older woman had done her best to hold up under all this, but—

"Of course not." Buck's voice was unexpectedly gentle as he bent over her. "I wouldn't expect you to do that. It's just that after making sure your home was safe from eavesdropping, it seemed a good place to discuss our next moves."

Mrs. H. looked up. "You're very kind, young man— especially since I don't believe this is the usual way you do business."

Buck stared down at her, speechless, as she summoned up a weak smile. "Not that I don't appreciate it. But if you need to be tough to find out who killed my brother, feel free to be as tough as you need to be." She straightened up. "Chris was killed over that painting he stole. I'm sure of that. If you need to find the picture to force whoever killed Chris into the open, you do that, too."

"We'll do our best, Mrs. H.," Liza promised.

"That's right," Michael added.

"Count on it," Buck rumbled.

They went outside to Buck's rental car. "So," Buck asked, "you want to be navigator?"

"I want to use the bathroom," she confessed. "But I hated the idea of ruining our dramatic exit by asking to use the one at Mrs. H.'s."

"Okay, bathroom break," Buck looked over at Michael.

"I'm good," Michael assured him.

"Better to make sure before we go," Buck said severely. "And if I hear one 'Are we there yet?' " from the backseat, you're walking home, young man.

"There speaks the father of the year," Liza muttered, leading the way back to her house.

Soon enough they were on the road. The drive down to Otis went by pretty unremarkably. The 101 was the big artery through the area, the first to be cleared of snow and any fallen trees. Buck drove his unfamiliar vehicle with authority, but without maniac speed. In about forty-five minutes, they arrived in the town of Otis, trying to track down the address Buck had given to Liza. "There's a map in the glove compartment," he said.

The address they were looking for was on a street of good-sized, well-kept houses. "There," Liza said, pointing. Buck pulled over, and they all got out.

"Do we need to come up with some sort of approach here?" Michael asked.

Buck shook his head. "I think we just go in straight, asking about Dalen." He paused. "We could mention the sister— Mrs. H., was it?"

"Elise Halvorsen," Liza said.

"Right." Buck led the way up the short walk and knocked on the door. It opened to reveal a man probably a few years older than Mrs. H., tall, slightly stooped. His white hair was cut short and his face was attractive, lined and creased in a way that Liza associated with outdoorsmen.

This could be Kevin in about thirty-five years, she

thought, looking at the squint lines around the man's eyes. She noticed there were also laugh lines around his mouth.

"Mister Partland?" Michael asked.

"That's me," the man replied.

Buck brought out his wallet. "I'm a private investigator—"

The open expression on Lewis Partland's face abruptly shut down. "If you're from that damned jackass on the phone, I already told him to go to hell."

"Whoa!" Liza called out to the closing door. "What jackass?"

"The jackass that just called a few minutes ago," Partland replied. "Tarleton, I think he said his name was."

"We're definitely *not* with him," Liza assured the old lawyer.

"Oh, you're some other bunch. Treasure hunters?" His brown eyes might be surrounded by wrinkles, but they were direct and clear as they took Liza in. "At least you're more polite and better looking than the jackass."

"I'm a neighbor of Elise Halvorsen's," Liza said. "She was Chris Dalen's sister."

"His sister Elise," Partland said. "Yes, he used to talk about her." He shook his head. "I read about Chris in the papers. That was a bad business."

"Tell me about it," Liza's response was heartfelt. "I found the body."

"You're the sudoku lady!" Partland said suddenly. "I've seen your picture in the paper. And I love your column. I'm working on one of those idiot books right now where they give you a suggested time limit."

He looked disgusted. "You should write a book and not waste time on wild-goose chases. Leave it to that Tarleton guy. He sounded like a prime variety of jackass— the rich kind. Told me there was money in it for me if I gave him what he wanted. When I told him I didn't want his money, he turned nasty. Started explaining to me as if I were simpleminded that he was an important man, and that there would be serious consequences if I didn't get in line."

Partland's broad, stooped shoulders rose and fell. "I own the house free and clear and have enough to live on—"

He broke off. "You don't need to hear that, or bother with looking for something that's lost and gone."

"We're just trying to help Mrs. Halvorsen get through a tough time," Liza told him. "Chris was supposed to come and stay with her after he was released. This whole thing has been a shock for her."

"She was the only one Chris worried over." A reminiscent look came over Partland's wrinkled features. "Said she was married to some big glom who wouldn't even let her speak to him."

He stepped aside from the door. "Well, come in, come in. As my dear wife used to say, no use letting all the heat out of the house."

It wasn't all that warm inside. Liza noticed that Partland wore a thick sweater. He brought them into the living room and indicated some seats, then settled into the big, battered armchair that was obviously his domain. "I don't know that there's much I can tell your neighbor." He shot a sharp glance over at Buck. "And not a damned thing I can say about that Mondrian."

Partland sighed. "I told him from the beginning there wasn't much I could do for him. There was an inside man—a guy who worked for the museum and gave him alarm codes and stuff. They got on to him quickly, and he squealed. Instead of getting rid of everything the way he was supposed to, the idiot even kept some tools. Some of them even had Dalen's fingerprints on them. The only way to get out from under this would have meant giving up the Mondrian, and Chris flat-out refused even to consider that."

"He was a very stubborn guy," Liza said.

The lawyer nodded vigorously. "I thought he was going to fire me for pressing the issue of returning the picture. Instead, he just went to insisting that he was innocent. Tried to concoct himself an alibi, but the heat was on. None of his associates wanted to be caught out in the spotlight with him."

"Did you know any of his associates?" Buck asked offhandedly.

That earned him another sharp glance from Partland. "In my line of work, I got to know a lot of what they now call 'career criminals.' Dalen was one of the more benign examples. He might have to crack safes or locks, but he never cracked anyone's head when he stole something."

The lawyer sighed. "Chris just pleaded innocent and watched the ship go down. Like I said, the thing that worried him most was how his big sister would take it."

He spread his hands. "Now, I've had an interesting stroll down memory line, but it's like I told that knucklehead on the phone. I didn't now what happened with the picture all those years ago, and I haven't heard anything since."

They thanked Partland, got in Buck's car, and headed back to Maiden's Bay.

"Oh, this is great," Michael said sourly. "What did that guy call us? Treasure hunters?"

"That's what this thing has turned into—a treasure hunt," Liza disgustedly agreed. "And the other teams are snagging clues ahead of us."

She turned to Buck, who had said nothing. But she saw he had his cop face working overtime. "I tried digging for Partland, but he pretty much dropped off the map after he retired." Buck's hands were tight on the steering wheel, as if he hoped to squeeze an answer out of it. "But it was Michelle who turned up an address for the guy. She really had to work her sources."

"So?" Michael asked.

"I could imagine Carlowe getting to Partland first. I'm not on good terms with most of my old LAPD colleagues, while Rod always knew where to spread the graft. Even that insurance investigator—"

"Howard Frost," Liza filled in the name.

Buck nodded. "I could see him tracking Partland down." But Tarleton?"

"Well, we know he wasn't bugging our meeting," Michael said facetiously.

But Buck nodded again, grimly literal. "The information was leaked."

"You can't be saying—" Liza began.

Buck's face remained stony. "Unless your pal Mrs. H. is on Tarleton's payroll, the only other possible leak is your friend Kevin."

They drove the next few miles in silence as she slowly digested the idea and got angrier and angrier. "The next exit is for Killamook," she said. "Get off the highway there."

Following Liza's directions, they soon pulled up in front of the Killamook Inn. Stepping into the reception area, Liza found John the assistant manager behind the desk. "Is Kevin around?" she asked, fighting to keep her voice mild.

"He's in his office," John replied, reaching for the phone.

"Don't call him," Liza said. "Let's make this a surprise."

Kevin's office held a lot of mementos from his days as a guide—fishing rods, hand-carved duck decoys, and of course his grandfather's bear rug. It also held a good-sized desk, a couple of comfortable armchairs for visitors, and a big leather executive chair where Kevin sat, going over some paperwork.

He looked up in surprise as his uninvited guests walked in. "Liza! What—?"

"No," she said, "the question is 'Why?' Why did you take the information about Lewis Partland straight from our meeting to Fritz Tarleton?"

Kevin dropped the papers and stared at his slightly messy desktop. "I—" he began, then stopped.

"Let's see if I can fill in the blank," Buck said quietly. "Lewis Partland gave a quick rundown on Tarleton's methods. First he offered you money. Then he tried threats."

Slowly, Kevin nodded. "Remember how he asked to see me when I brought you to dinner, Liza? That was the money offer. He told me he was meeting with Chris Dalen later that night and he wanted it kept private."

Kevin let out a long breath. "From there, the veiled threats started."

"I remember you talking about how important Tarleton could be to the inn during dinner," Liza said.

"He's been putting the screws to me for two days, talking about recommendations for the owners of the inn. I've put years into building up this place. My job is on the line."

"That sucks." Michael spoke from experience. He'd had scripting jobs scuttled by producers or backers throwing their weight around.

"Tarleton knew this was my first management job. His security guy—McShane—had a whole dossier on me." Kevin glanced over at Liza. "He had one on you, too, and he was convinced that you would start poking around in this case. So he wanted the inside track."

His hands knotted together on the desktop. "I was desperate, so I decided to throw him a bone. I told him about that retired lawyer."

"So Tarleton made a phone call, and Partland nearly slammed the door in our faces," Buck said.

Kevin looked over at the detective. "I figured if the old guy knew anything, he'd have said spoken up already."

Buck glanced at Liza and Michael. "That is a point."

"The real point of this is that you should have told us what Tarleton was doing," Liza said.

"What good would that have done?" Kevin's voice sounded tired.

"I'll show you." Liza reached for the phone. "Mind if I make a long-distance call?"

In moments she heard a voice announcing, "M-Markson Associates."

Another temp, Liza thought, *and one who won't last very long.*

"Liza Kelly for Michelle, please," she said.

"I—I don't—" the stammering voice replied.

"Just tell her who's calling. Liza Kelly," Liza repeated. "And if she fires you, well, look on the bright side. You'll be out of there."

"You're right." At least the voice stopped stammering. Liza found herself briefly on hold, then heard Michelle's voice.

"What's the news?" her partner wanted to know.

"We talked to Lewis Partland, and I'm afraid he wasn't much help. But something else came up." Liza gave a brief rundown on what had being going on between Tarleton and Kevin.

"I don't like people who use crude blackmail," Michelle said.

That's because you use it so much more subtly—and effectively, Liza silently commented.

"However—" Michelle drew out the word, something she usually did when coming to a decision. "Maybe we can show Mr. Tarleton the error of his ways. Can you put this on the speaker?"

Luckily, Kevin's phone was equipped with this feature.

"Buck," Michelle asked, "what was the name of that unsuitable boyfriend Ritz Tarleton picked up? Tinsel?"

"Tyndal," Buck replied. "Small-time grifter and provider of recreational chemicals for the celebutante crowd."

"More like celebri*tart*," Michelle said. "Mr. Tyndal is also something of an amateur filmmaker. He and Ritz Tarleton made a rather boring sex video."

"That would explain why Daddy had a whole can of whup-ass opened on him," Michael muttered.

"It's stayed under the radar so far," Michelle went on, "but I've got a copy. Thought it might come in handy to make a good splashy distraction if the media ever really got after one of our clients. You can tell Mr. Tarleton that if he doesn't see the error of his ways, he'll get to see some tamer excerpts tonight on *Evening Celebrity News*."

"I could be wrong here, but I think you really don't like this guy," Michael spoke up.

"Oh, please," Michelle replied. "He's just a travel agent with delusions of grandeur. His father came home from World War II with the bright idea of selling package tours. Then Fritz—and what kind of name is that, anyway?—just picked the right time to go into the deluxe travel business. Just because he was making arrangements for the rich and famous, he thought he'd become one of them. With that daughter of his, though, it looks as if they'll go from shirt-sleeves to shirtsleeves in three generations."

"You know, Michelle," Liza said, "it sounds to me as if you would enjoy the chance to put Mr. Tarleton in his place."

"Mmmmm-yes," Michelle's voice turned very sweet—always a danger sign in conversations with her. "You're far too nice to do this job effectively. Is Tarleton still at the—what is the ridiculous name of that inn again."

"The Killamook Inn." Liza did her best to keep a straight face as Kevin flinched at that comment. "Do you need the number?"

"No, we've got it here," Michelle said. "I even stayed there, remember. Very nice place, in spite of that name."

They exchanged good-byes, and Liza cut the connection. "Well, that should provide some counterpressure."

"If you consider being hit on the head by a falling piano counterpressure," Michael said.

"I think Fritz Tarleton will back off," Liza told Kevin.

He looked a little dazed. "I don't know how—" His thanks were interrupted by a knock on the office door.

"Come in," Kevin called.

John the assistant manager opened the door and stepped in, an envelope in his hand. "We were just going through the mail delivery, and this came in."

Kevin extended his hand, but John offered the envelope to Liza. She looked at the scrawled inscription.

LIZA KELLY
c/o The Killamook Inn

"Now what the hell is this?" she asked.

PART THREE:
Coloring

Some sudoku can actually be solved in your head. Most, however, require the use of a pencil to list the candidates for each space and slowly reduce them. For some solvers, though, tackling more esoteric puzzles means bringing *pencils*, plural, to the job.

The idea is to map out competing chains of logic by filling the spaces involved with different colors. It's a technique that can be useful, and at times it turns a plain old sudoku into a piece of modern art.

And unless you know the logic behind it, coloring is about as easy to understand as modern art, too.

—Excerpt from *Sudo-cues* by Liza K

12

Kevin looked more intently at the envelope Liza was tearing open. "That's Killamook Inn stationery."

John nodded. "It just made a round trip between here and the post office."

One of the two pieces of paper inside the envelope was inn stationery, too. Liza frowned as she read the scribbled words:

Liza,

Maybe I'm just in a blue funk. Or maybe, if I'm not around to pick this up from you, it will turn out that I was right when I spoke tonight about the dangers of do-it-yourself art dealing—at least with stolen Mondrians.

Hey, I'm a big boy. I know what I'm getting into, here. If things go wrong, one of the things I'll really miss would be the look on your face discovering I'd be your next-door neighbor.

My sister is a good woman. She told me a lot about you—how you cracked two murder cases. I know it's a lot to ask, but if things go wrong, I hope you'll help

Elise to find the painting. I know she's having money troubles these days. Maybe getting the reward from the insurance company will help to make up for some of the grief I've caused her over the years.

If you can put this over, at least I'll know that I was able to help Elise.

The note was signed "Chris Dalen."

After she read it aloud, Michael crossed his arms. "*He* doesn't ask for much, this guy."

Kevin managed a ghost of a laugh. "He's not asking for anything that Liza isn't already doing—with our help."

Michael shot him a glance. "More or less."

Liza barely paid attention as the sniping resumed. She was busy examining the other piece of paper that came from the envelope. This wasn't stationery. It was some kind of art paper, translucent vellum. As for the geometric design drawn on it—

"What's that?" Buck Foreman asked, looking over her shoulder.

"It's a very nice miniature copy of *Composition in Blue, Red, and Green*." She recognized it from the faded magazine page tacked up on the wall of Patrician Books. "How thoughtful of Chris to send along a reproduction of the painting I'm supposed to find."

"It's a nice job," Buck said. "Ink and watercolor."

"Lovely." Liza's voice was sour. "I suppose if I screw up on finding the painting, I can always have this framed and give it to Mrs. H."

She glanced over at the assistant manager, who was trying to retreat to the door. "I suppose I should say thank you, John." Then she looked at Buck, Michael, and Kevin. "Otherwise—well, I guess our business here is done."

Liza felt Kevin's eyes on her back as she walked out of the office. She glanced back from the doorway. Yes, Kevin was looking at her. His mouth opened and then clamped shut in a tight line.

Yeah, Liza thought, *nothing much we can say right now.*

She tucked the note and the picture back in the envelope, put the envelope in her pocket, and left.

They drove back to Maiden's Bay. As they headed up Main Street, Liza's stomach suddenly growled. Putting a hand firmly over the noisemaker, she asked, "What do you say to a late lunch at Ma's Café?"

"That's why I go on business trips," Buck said, "for the cushy expense account meals."

He found a parking space, and they crossed Main to enter the café. The combination of steam and fried food filled Liza's nostrils, and all of a sudden she found herself salivating. The booths that lined the walls were pretty much empty—most of the regulars had finished their lunches by now. A few of the older habitués lined the lunch counter, hunched over cups of coffee. Liza wondered if some of them ever went home. The only place she saw them was at the counter at Ma's.

Buck led the way to the back booth, seating himself so he had a clear view of the door.

Some habits die hard, Liza thought as she shepherded Michael into the inside seat. He was right-handed while she was a lefty, so she wanted the outside seat. Otherwise, as bitter experience had shown, trying to eat side by side would result in a case of dueling elbows.

Liz Sanders, sister of the original Ma of Ma's Café, came to take their orders. Buck had the Yankee pot roast, Michael had the artery buster, and Liza ended up with the salad with grilled chicken—honey Dijon dressing on the side.

They had just started eating when Liza heard the door open behind her. Buck sat up straighter. "Somebody's coming our way."

The first thing Liza noticed was the shiny brown polyester parka. "Could I speak with you for a moment?" Howard Frost asked.

Stuck with a mouthful of lettuce, Liza had no graceful way of saying "no."

"I know we got off to a bad start." Frost's jowls wobbled apologetically as he spoke. "It's just that this whole thing with the Mondrian has hung over my head for the past dozen years. I'm a good investigator, have a damned good track record. But that painting—not recovering it has been the big failure of my career."

A multimillion-dollar failure—guess I'd get kind of excited over it if it were me, Liza thought.

"My neighbor mentioned that every time Chris Dalen came up for parole, you'd turn up at the hearing to argue against it," she said.

A flash of fire came to Frost's eyes. "Damned right. They tell us that prison is for rehabilitation. You get out early if you show you've changed your ways—"

Buck cleared his throat as if something had gone down the wrong way. Frost flashed him a conspiratorial smile. "I'd guess you work or have worked in law enforcement," he said, "but I'm talking about theory here—your practical viewpoint may be somewhat different."

He turned back to Liza. "So, if Dalen had become an honest man who should leave prison early, wouldn't surrendering what he stole be the honest thing to do?"

"He was in prison more than a decade," Liza began.

"Sitting on his tail, waiting to sell that Mondrian. I worked my tail off the same number of years, but I'm not getting a three-million-dollar retirement package."

"You're not dead, either—Dalen was murdered, after all," Liza pointed out, although she had to admit, Frost did have a point. But she still wasn't going to share any information with the investigator—such as Chris Dalen's posthumous letter.

One of the regulars at the lunch counter suddenly spun on his stool to point at Frost. "You're the insurance guy from W.A.G., ain'tcha?"

"Western Assurance Group," Frost said politely.

"Y'know, I got some storm damage to my house after that big blow the other night." The coffee drinker's Adam's apple bobbed up and down on his scrawny throat. "I hope you ain't going to screw me over like you did to Elise Halvorsen."

"I can assure you," Frost began, but the other guy cut him off.

"I've known Elise for about forty years—you I know for about fifteen seconds. I dunno about 'resting assured,' but I know whose word I'd trust." With that, the local spun back to his coffee.

Frost contented himself with giving cards to Buck and Michael. He asked Liza whether she still had the one he'd given her, and then he left.

"You think he got the idea he wasn't wanted?" Michael asked, deadpan.

They managed to finish their meal without incident, and Buck gave them a lift back to Hackleberry Avenue. "I'll have to push it a bit to catch my flight back to L.A." So he just said good-bye and took off.

Michael glanced over at Liza's house.

"I'm going to be working," she warned.

He nodded. "I guess Mrs. H. could use some company, anyway."

Arriving back home, Liza disappointed Rusty by heading straight for her computer instead of the treats jar. She sat down and forced herself to crank out a simple puzzle before taking another shot at beaming an IM to Uncle Jim. Liza hoped he was around this time because she really needed his help with Dalen's seventeen clue sudoku.

Luckily, a response appeared in the box on her screen.

Hi Liza, Uncle Jim typed. **That was a pretty interesting sudoku, considering it came out of an introductory class.**

Even as she read, Liza was typing herself. **Do you see any hint of a message in there?**

For a long moment she got no response. Then words began to appear.

With any kind of secret message, there has to be some shared system between the sender and the receiver. For instance, a codebook allows someone to transform words into

5	8			7			6	9
	7		8	3	9		1	
			5					
		8				2		
4			6		5			7
		6				1		
				9				
	4		5	6	8		7	
3	6			1			8	4

groups of letters or numbers, and to turn them back. A cipher key lets the same thing happen, translating messages letter by letter. If there's a message in the puzzle you sent, we don't have whatever it takes to turn it out.

Liza's heart sank as she read. This was what she was afraid she'd hear.

We discussed this the last time you came to me to crack a cipher.

She leaned over her keyboard. I know. I was just hoping you could surprise me. Run your magic eyes over it and see something I could not.

Uncle Jim's answer appeared. Your confidence in me is very flattering . . . misplaced, maybe, but flattering.

After a moment, more words crept onto the screen. You still there, Liza? I didn't hurt your feelings, did I?

Liza was busy typing. No, there's just more. I got a letter from the dead man today. He asked me to help find the hidden painting. Here's what he said:

The next part she had to type very carefully. She wanted an exact transcription of Chris Dalen's note.

After she sent that, Liza typed, **When he asks me to go for the picture, he seems to think I'll have no trouble finding it. Is there something in the letter that I'm missing?**

His answer seemed equally puzzled. **That's all it says?**

"Well, it's on a piece of hotel stationery," Liza muttered. She typed that in, adding, **so it has the address of the Killamook Inn.**

Another brief pause. **There could be some sort of secret writing involved. That would involve chemical analysis. Or . . . it could be simply mechanical, say an overlay with cutouts so that only certain words come through.**

Liza began typing excitedly. **He did include a copy of the Mondrian painting. It's on very fine paper, almost see-through.**

The answer came just as quickly. **Try plaicing it over the note—rigth now!** Uncle Jim was usually a careful typist. The typos must indicate that he was excited.

This may take a little while, Liza typed. She spread out the note and then the miniature painting. It was a lot smaller, half the size of the notepaper. She lined up the two upper left corners, squinted through the translucent paper . . . and didn't find anything that made sense. She turned the painting upside down, then at a right angle, and then turned that upside down. Nothing.

Liza did the same thing at each corner of the notepaper. Steadily using more bad words to vent her growing frustration, she went through the process all over again, this time aligning the edge of the art reproduction with the text.

Slamming both pieces of paper down, she turned back to the keyboard. **I couldn't get a coherent communication—or even complete words. The message is scribbled. It's as if the tip of the pen never left the paper. And each line runs off at an angle.**

Liza described everything she'd done. **But I can't even get anything to line up.**

Scribbled . . . The words stayed on the screen for a while. Then a block of text appeared very quickly.

Sounds as if this note was written in a hurry. What if there's something missing? Maybe Chris Dalen intended to pass along that missing piece of the puzzle and died before he managed to do that.

Liza began typing even as she read. **Great idea, Uncle Jim. I have to bring this note to the sheriff anyway. Maybe I can get a look at Dalen's belongings.**

An answer came almost as quickly. **Remember, the killer might have taken whatever it was.**

Liza typed back, **Unless it was something Dalen got in his few hours of freedom, it had to be something he had in prison. I just hope I get lucky and identify it.**

She thanked her uncle, logged off, and gathered up the note, the picture, and the envelope. Then she shrugged into her coat, got in her car, and headed back downtown. Although the clock said late afternoon, the overcast sky pretty emphatically said night. The guys at Castelli's Market had finished with the dinner rush and were getting ready to close up when Liza popped in and used their coin-operated copy machine.

The sheriff will probably take the originals, she thought. *Better get a copy of everything.*

Main Street was pretty quiet as she parked. At City Hall, the deputy on duty told her that Sheriff Clements wasn't in. "We've got that statie in his office, though," the officer said.

"Detective Everard?"

The deputy nodded. "I can call back and see if he wants to talk to you."

Moments later Liza entered the office/interrogation room. Ted Everard looked up almost warily from the desk, where he was apparently filling in some sort of form. "You wanted to see the sheriff?"

"I was up at the Killamook Inn today, and this came in the

mail for me." She handed over all of Chris Dalen's posthumous post.

Everard used his pen to open the note on the desk. "Let me guess," he said. "All your friends had to touch this, too?"

"I suppose so," Liza admitted as the detective transferred each item to a separate plastic evidence bag. She mentioned Uncle Jim's suggestion about the possibility of secret writing.

"So now we're going from cheap detective fiction to spy novels, are we?" Everard paused. "Or is this the uncle that Clements told me about—the spy?"

"I can't say," Liza replied stiffly. "I've never asked."

"And I suppose he'd never tell." Everard gave her a wry smile, and Liza found herself relaxing a bit.

"I thought one thing in that letter was kind of weird. He asks me to help Mrs. Halvorsen find the painting—"

"First decent thing I've heard about him," Everard said.

"But he just seems to take it for granted that I'd find it," Liza finished.

Everard shrugged. "Maybe he had a higher estimation of your detective abilities than I—" He broke off. "Than other people do," he ended somewhat lamely.

"Suppose there was something else, some clue, and he never made it to me to pass it along," Liza said.

"Well, there were no maps, no detailed sets of instructions, nothing in his address book with a star or a dollar sign beside it." Everard got up. "At this point, I'd be glad for a map of Oregon with a circle and a note saying, 'Somewhere around here.'"

"You're that hot to recover the Mondrian?" Liza asked.

"Only as it relates to the murder," Everard said. "If we find someone digging it up, chances are we've also caught whoever killed Dalen."

"I hadn't thought of it that way," she admitted.

"Well, I have, and that's why I figure it wouldn't hurt to sit here with you and go over his personal effects." Everard stepped away. A moment later he returned with a large cardboard box.

"There's not much," he warned. "It's not as though you go into the joint with a trunk full of belongings." There was a small suitcase, a package of underwear, socks, a new shirt still in its plastic wrap. It even had a price tag from a chain store stuck on.

"He picked this stuff up in Portland," Everard said.

From his prison days, Dalen had some sort of handmade arts-and-crafts piece of art—perhaps a gift for his sister. And there was a dog-eared copy of a book on sudoku. Liza made a mental note of that. She had the same book at home and could check against Chris's sudoku puzzle to see if it was some sort of book code.

"This is the stuff Dalen had on him." Everard held up an envelope marked PERSONAL EFFECTS and spilled it onto the desk. Liza saw a handkerchief, some change, a wallet, and a ring of keys.

"The wallet has a bunch of expired cards—credit, library, driver's license," Everard told her. "No photographs, no written material. As for the keys . . ." he shook his head. "God knows what they open."

Liza stared down at the little pile.

"Not much in the way of clues," Everard said.

She nodded. "Not much in the way of a life."

The police-band radio in a corner of the room suddenly crackled. "Car two," an excited voice came over. "We got a dead one—"

A new, older-sounding voice came on. "Ah, control, that's a ten forty-nine." The voice went on to give an address. Everard repacked the box. "I'll have to go over there."

"Another example of major crime?" Liza tried to joke, but Everard definitely wasn't laughing.

Well, she thought, *if crime stats are his life . . .*

Everard flew off. Liza left City Hall more slowly. By the time she reached her car, though, she'd come to a decision.

The address from the police scanner was a small strip mall on the way back to Killamook. The place had a reputation as bad-luck retail space—stores there opened and promptly went out of business. As she pulled up, she saw that half of the storefronts were empty. A rental car stood in what would have been a dim corner, except that now two police cruisers were shining their headlights on it.

The glow also illuminated another rental car. Liza braked sharply as she recognized Alvin Hunzinger, lawyer to the stars, being very messily sick on the front fender.

"Alvin! Alvin, are you all right?" Liza rushed over to the pudgy lawyer. A second later, she felt about ready to add to the mess on Alvin's fender.

Liza had finally noticed the man sprawled at a crazy angle across the backseat of the other car. He had very broad shoulders, and a face like a lizard—a rather surprised lizard.

The guy exactly matched Buck Foreman's description of Rod Carlowe—except for what looked like a small bullet hole in his forehead.

13

Liza took Alvin by the arm, turning him away from the mess on his fender—not to mention the one in the other car. The pudgy little man was shaking, and he leaned heavily on Liza for a couple of steps.

Ted Everard suddenly appeared beside them. "What are *you* doing here?" he demanded in barely restrained fury.

"I thought I would drive by and see what was up," Liza replied. "And I saw a friend in trouble. Are you okay, Alvin? Can I get you anything?" she asked.

Like, say, a lawyer? she asked inside her head.

"A sip of water might be nice." Alvin was still a bit green in the face, but he seemed to be recovering himself.

Liza gave Alvin's arm to Everard. "Don't let him fall," she warned. "He's obviously had a nasty shock."

The detective looked as if he'd like to step after her—probably with the intention of strangling her—but Alvin stumbled. So Everard got to stand fuming, supporting the guy he probably thought of as his prime suspect, while Liza ran to her car for a water bottle.

"It's been sitting in the car for a while," she warned. "So it's pretty cold."

Alvin twisted off the cap, brought the bottle to his lips, and tipped it back. He swished water around in his mouth and spat it out. When he went to hand the bottle back to her, Liza shook her head. "Alvin, it's all yours."

"Thanks," he muttered, and then shuddered. "I had just found the—the—Carlowe—when the first police car arrived. There's a difference between examining even the most grisly crime-scene photos and seeing the real thing."

Liza's stomach squirmed in sympathy. "I know what you mean," she said fervently.

Another police cruiser pulled up, and Sheriff Clements stepped out. He didn't look in the best of moods, either. "I hope that isn't our guest of honor, not after that rookie reported a DB in the clear and Walters backed him up."

Everard shook his head. "Nah. We got one in the back of the tan Taurus. And this gentleman was discovered on the scene."

"Alvin Hunzinger," Alvin said, extending his hand.

"We've met before." Clements did not take up the offer of a handshake.

That's right, Liza thought. *Michelle dragged Alvin up here when she was being questioned about the murder during the filming in Maiden's Bay.*

Oddly enough, the sudden hostility from the police seemed to act as a tonic on the little lawyer. Alvin stood straighter and spoke more clearly. "The man in the Taurus is Rod Carlowe, a private investigator working for my law firm. He'd asked for a face-to-face meeting, and when I arrived, I found . . . what you see." He shuddered again, losing some of his lawyerly assurance.

"Single gunshot in the forehead," Everard reported. "Body's still warm."

"Through and through?" Clements asked.

"No exit wound, so the bullet is probably still in the

skull. The entrance wound is small—probably a twenty-two or twenty-five caliber."

The sheriff grunted. "Sounds like a Saturday night special."

Then his eye fell on the two eavesdroppers. "I think that's enough for now." He leaned down to Alvin. "Mr. Hunzinger, we need a statement from you. Do you feel well enough to come down to the station and give it?"

"Of course I'll be glad to assist the authorities." Hunzinger looked about as enthusiastic as a man being invited for a session of root canal.

Clements rolled his eyes. He looked just as eager to tangle with a celebrity lawyer. "And Liza?"

Everard's lips compressed into a thin line. "She came up shortly after I arrived."

The sheriff glanced over at Liza's car. "You get yourself a police band radio installed?"

"Ms. Kelly was down at the station turning in some evidence when she overheard the call," Everard said stiffly.

Sheriff Clements looked at his colleague, a grin threatening to subvert the detached expression Liza considered his "cop face."

"And you didn't caution her about interfering?"

Everard's lips got tighter. "I didn't think it necessary with a reasonable member of the public." His voice grew grim. "I'll know better in the future."

"I wasn't interfering," Liza protested. "As I told Detective Everard, I drove past, saw a friend, and went to help."

Clements turned to Alvin. "Do you feel as if you need any further help, Mr. Hunzinger?"

"Ah—no, no," Alvin hurriedly said. His plump face quivered as he shook his head. Whether that was from his quick movement or his terror at Michelle's reaction if he got her partner dragged in for questioning, Liza couldn't quite tell.

"In that case, Ms. Kelly, I think you're done here." Sheriff Clements had his official voice back, and there was no arguing with that.

Besides, I don't need to be there while Alvin spars with the cops, she thought. *If he's done that once, he's probably done that a thousand times.*

"Okay, Sheriff," she said meekly and headed back to her car, thinking over what she'd overheard.

Everard reported that the body was still warm. Although creepy, that was a good thing. Considering the bad blood between Buck Foreman and Rod Carlowe, it really was for the best that Buck had left town during the afternoon. He couldn't be considered a suspect.

Holding on to that comforting thought, Liza drove home. She'd barely gotten out of her car when Mrs. Halvorsen's door flew open.

But it wasn't Mrs. H. framed in the lights of the entranceway. Instead, Michael peered out at her. "The TV news just had a special report. Rod Carlowe is—"

"Dead," Liza finished. "I know. I was there."

Mrs. H. appeared beside Michael. "We were going to invite you over for supper, but you were gone. Have you eaten, dear? Michael, why don't you bring her some leftovers?" Moments later Michael appeared at Liza's door, bearing a covered dish wrapped in a towel. Rusty was already sniffing the air eagerly, his tail wagging.

"Let's sit at the kitchen table," Liza suggested. She put a hand to her stomach. That lunch salad suddenly seemed like part of the distant past. In spite of the shocks she'd encountered at the murder scene—or maybe because of them—she was hungry.

At least she was until Michael removed the cover to reveal a supper of meatballs and spaghetti with lots of piping-hot, steaming tomato sauce.

"Gurk!" Liza said, her hand flying to her mouth. "That's not exactly what you want to see after stumbling across someone who's been shot in the head."

Michael hurriedly covered the plate again. "Oh, man, I hadn't thought of that. Was it bad?"

"Actually, it was pretty neat." Liza paused. "That's 'neat' as in 'not messy,' not 'neat' as in 'really enjoyable.'"

Michael looked surprised. "I'd think a shooting like that would be fairly messy."

Liza shook her head. "They said the bullet stayed in the skull. Just a little hole—a twenty-two caliber, I think Ted Everard said."

"Professional assassins use that size bullet. It works well with a silencer." He saw the look she was giving him and shrugged. "Hey, I write mystery stories. I'm supposed to know this sort of stuff."

"I don't think Sheriff Clements thinks that way." Liza tried to dredge up exactly what the sheriff and Everard had said. "It could have been a twenty-two or a twenty-five caliber. Clements said it sounded like a Saturday night special."

"Yeah, there are a lot of cheap guns made in low calibers like that—street guns, usually involved in street crime. I can't imagine there's a lot of that in Maiden's Bay."

"Well, there was a terrible rash of jack-o-lantern thefts around Halloween," Liza told him. "But I don't remember any of them being taken at gunpoint."

"Let's go back to the MOM equation. We've got another murder happening just days after Chris Dalen was killed," Michael said.

"So it's likely the two deaths are connected," Liza agreed. "Especially since Rod Carlowe is one of the people actively looking for the painting that Chris Dalen hid."

"People are getting a little crazy about that," Michael admitted. "Mrs. H. told me she had to chase some nut with a shovel out of her backyard this afternoon."

"It's a shame we don't have pictures of all the people involved in this treasure hunt. Maybe the guy she chased off was Carlowe—or Fritz Tarleton."

Michael laughed. "I can't imagine Tarleton with anything

as plebeian as a shovel in his hands." He grew more serious. "Or a Saturday night special, if it comes to that. Vinnie Tanino, well, maybe. You could imagine him getting hold of a cheap, hard-to-trace gun."

"You suggested that a hit man might use a twenty-two," Liza pointed out.

She paused for a moment. "Do you think someone like Alvin Hunzinger could get a gun like that?"

Now it was Michael's turn to look at her. "Why would the lawyer to the stars be going to town with a Saturday night special?"

"He was there, too, barfing all over his car." All of a sudden, Liza got an errant whiff of meatballs and sauce—and her own stomach began to get queasy again.

"Well, that doesn't exactly sound like the actions of a cold-blooded killer." Michael shrugged, his hands palms up. "For that matter, Carlowe used to be a cop, where he could have come across an arsenal's worth of street weapons. A crooked cop, especially, would have uses for an untraceable gun. Suppose he brought along a small pocket piece for protection, but then the killer somehow got hold of it—"

"Well, that pretty much rules out means. Any of our suspects could have shot him then." Liza leaned back in her kitchen chair. "I don't think we're going to get very far with opportunity. The police will have to check out alibis. What about motive?"

"It looks as though this treasure hunt has gotten deadly serious," Michael said.

"Does it have to connect to the hunt after all?" Liza suddenly asked.

"I suppose Carlowe could have insulted somebody's wife, and they went home to get the gun they keep in the dresser drawer." Michael made a face. "But it seems awfully coincidental."

"No, no." Liza made pushing-away gestures. "What if there was some sort of side deal? Buck told us that Car-

lowe wasn't above using blackmail. Suppose he had something on Tarleton—like that sex tape of his daughter's? We
know that Pops Tarleton was ready to go to extremes for
Ritz. He had that boyfriend beaten up."

"Funny you didn't mention that to Michelle earlier today," Michael said.

"We were trying to make Tarleton back off—he was doing the wrong thing, putting pressure on Kevin," Liza said.
"Michelle has a reputation for being tough but fair. Compare that to what we've heard about Rod Carlowe."

"Okay, okay," Michael frowned. "But if Tarleton runs
true to *his* reputation, he'd have passed the job on to his security guy, Jim McShane."

"Another former cop who could have gotten hold of a
street gun," Liza pointed out.

"Yeah, but it's one thing to order a beating put on someone, quite another to order a killing. If Tarleton wanted to
keep from being blackmailed by Carlowe, would he put
himself in the power of McShane? I don't think so."

"So who else might Carlowe have been trying to get
over on?" Liza asked. "Frankie Basso?"

"Trying to put the screws to Fat Frankie? I don't think
so—unless Carlowe had a bad case of death wish."

"Well," Liza pointed out, "that's what he got."

"And he was working for Conn Lezat." Michael stopped.
"Unless Carlowe was running a scam on his own client."

"A stand-up guy like Rod Carlowe? Perish the thought."
Liza's lightheartedly sarcastic expression faded. "Suppose
Carlowe was the one who killed Chris Dalen. But before
Dalen died, he gave away some information—maybe not
the location of the painting itself, but enough to put one of
the searchers ahead in the treasure hunt."

Michael slowly nodded. "How would he use that clue
for his own profit? If it's not conclusive, it might not lead
him to the Mondrian. Then Carlowe would have killed
Dalen for nothing. I suppose he might try to sell whatever
he got from Dalen. If it didn't pan out, well, caveat emptor."

" 'Let the buyer beware,' " Liza echoed. "Or he could have been holding up Lezat for more money."

"It's possible that he'd been spotted dealing with one of the other enemy camps. That would be taken as betraying Lezat," Michael pointed out.

Liza shook her head in disbelief. "And who would have seen that? Who's working for Lezat out here? Alvin Hunzinger? Can you really see him as the triggerman? Slamming people with legal paper, yes, he's good at that. But shooting someone? He caves when Michelle gives him a dirty look."

"Better men than he have done that," Michael said.

"Oh, come on," Liza argued. "It's like believing in the Killer Bunny Rabbit."

Michael only shrugged. "Fine. But rabbits have pretty sharp teeth."

Then that annoying little voice in the back of Liza's head chimed in. *And did you notice? Alvin was at the scene of the crime when the police arrived.*

14

Liza did her best to quash that aggravating voice by resolutely doing something practical. "I guess I should call Ava."

"That's right," Michael said. "You have another first-person report."

And you'll have to tell her about Alvin, that damned mental voice chimed in.

Liza put all her attention to calling up the *Oregon Daily*.

"Well, you're getting a bit better," Ava greeted her. "But the idea of working for a newspaper is that you're supposed to call the moment you see news, not sometime afterward."

Of course, Ava had her sources in the local force. Somebody would have seen Liza on the scene and let Ava know. "You're making me sorry I called in at all," Liza replied. "If you don't need my story—"

"To tell you the truth, I don't think we do this time around," Ava told her. "Sheriff Clements moved very quickly—Vinnie Tanino is already in custody."

"Tanino?" Liza glanced over at Michael, remembering his comment about professional assassins. Had Vinnie

Tanlines tried his luck as a hit man? "How did they get on to him so quickly?"

"I don't know how carefully you looked in the back of Carlowe's Taurus," Ava began.

"Not very," Liza said quickly. "He was lying there with a hole in his head."

"Well, besides Carlowe, there was a portable DVD player."

"Did they get a look at what was in it?" Liza asked, visions of Ritz Tarleton's scandalous sex antics turning up.

"No," Ava answered, "because nothing was in it. The player was lying there, open and empty, but the cops managed to lift a fingerprint off the Eject button. It didn't take them very long to discover that Tanino's right index finger was a perfect match."

"Bad news for Vinnie Tanlines," Liza said.

"But good news for us." Ava's voice took on a gloating tone. "This is well before the paper goes to press. We have time to design a killer front page and do the whole package. I had Murph working on a background piece about Tanino's criminal career just in case."

"Well, if you're happy, I'm happy," Liza told her. "Especially if you don't need anything from me."

"You're off the hook," Ava said. "But next time—"

"Right, right." Liza said some hasty good-byes and hung up. Then she turned to Michael and gave him the whole story.

"Well, Tanino didn't particularly strike me as a criminal genius," Michael said. "Now that they've got him for Carlowe's murder, they'll try all the harder to connect him to the Dalen case as well. I bet the sheriff is happy to wind up the local crime wave—what are you doing?" he interrupted himself as Liza hauled out her coat again.

"I'm going down to City Hall," she explained, pulling on the waxed jacket. "My friend Alvin is stuck down there." *And,* she thought, *I might get more of the story than I would talking to Ava—or reading her paper.*

Michael got his coat, and they both went out the door.

He stood on the path to Mrs. Halvorsen's house, waving as Liza drove off.

Most of the stores along Main Street were dark by now. Liza had an easy time parking, but she remained in her car, watching the front of City Hall. Other times she'd come here after a new development in a murder case to find a media circus in full cry. Tonight, though, there were only a couple of acts.

A chauffeured limo sat on the curb in front of the building, parked between two news vans. *Maybe Alvin has already arranged for a ride out of town,* Liza thought. Only one camera was actually out, busily recording a very thin, rather chilled-looking local reporter speaking in front of the building.

Why does she have to do that? Liza wondered. *Why not let her give her report in a nice, warm studio? Do they have to justify the cost of the vans and crews? Or is this how they tell all us couch potatoes that the station is always on the move, looking for news?*

By the time the young woman was done, her lips were blue as she climbed back into the van. Liza took advantage of the lull in the action to pull on an unflattering woolen hat and, using that as a camouflage, walk into City Hall.

Liza yanked off her disguise and stepped up to the duty desk. Despite her hat hair, the deputy behind the desk recognized her. So did Alvin Hunzinger, who waved to her from the bench where he was sitting with a man who looked like central casting's idea of a major executive, from the distinguished silver hair in the four-hundred-dollar coif to the camel-hair coat.

I guess he explains the limo outside. It would make the perfect prop for him, Liza's irreverent side suggested. Then she recognized the face atop all the other accoutrements. That was Fritz Tarleton, and he was trying to do some sort of deal with Alvin. The Tarleton behind Tarleton Tours gave Liza the kind of look his daughter reserved for those annoying little people. But Alvin rose and walked over to Liza.

"I hear you're off the hook for Carlowe's murder," she said with a smile.

He returned it. "As if there were any doubt. I did get to be the object of a spirited bidding war. Mr. Tarleton and that Tanino fellow were both interested in my services."

"I can understand why Tanino would want your services," Liza began.

"Even though he couldn't really afford them," Alvin said. "He tried to offer me a credit card with another name on it."

"But Tarleton?"

The lawyer shrugged. "He was concerned for his head of security, who is still inside with the forces of law and order."

"Why?" Liza asked. "I thought they had Tanino dead to rights."

"I'm afraid Mr. Tanino doesn't think so." Alvin raised a hand to his ear. As if on cue, Vinnie Tanino's voice echoed from the interrogation room in the rear. "I tolja, I didn't do nothing." There was a brief pause as someone else must have spoken—in a lower tone of voice.

"Yeah, awright, so I got into Carlowe's car. I mean, that PI's been nosin' around lookin' for the painting. I seen a chance to see what he'd got. How was I supposed to know there was a stiff in the back?"

Another brief pause was followed by an even more agitated outburst from Vinnie Tanlines. "Dammit, I looked in the DVD player after I checked Carlowe for a pulse. Had to take my glove off for that. He was gone, and the player was empty. So I got outta there—fast. But I did call you guys."

Liza stared at Alvin. "So, Tanino's going to try and fight it? Even though that fingerprint puts him right at the crime scene?"

Alvin shrugged. "In my professional opinion, the police have only a circumstantial case so far. Maybe they can develop more, but at this point, any competent attorney could get Mr. Tanino acquitted."

Liza would have liked to discuss that at more length. But this was the moment a large, pink-faced man emerged from the corridor leading to the interrogation room and the cells. He did a double take as he glanced over at the bench where Fritz Tarleton was sitting. "Boss! What are you doing here? You had that meeting up in Portland—"

"I cut it short when I heard about what happened here." Tarleton glanced into the rear area. "I hope it wasn't too much trouble for you."

The big man—Jim McShane, Liza realized—shrugged. "Pretty much the usual sort of questions that get asked in this sort of situation."

"So our . . . business continues," Tarleton said. It didn't take Derrick Robbins's cryptology library to decode that. Carlowe might be dead, Tanino in custody. But the treasure hunt goes on.

Tarleton turned to Alvin. "Do you need that lift, Hunzinger?"

Alvin shook his head. "I have a friend here to get me to my car." He stood with Liza until Tarleton and his security guy left together. "I'm sorry to impose on you, but I get tired of people waving wads of money at me and expecting me to sit up and bark."

"Tarleton thought he could buy you?" Liza blinked in disbelief. "I've never heard of you letting down a client."

Alvin gave her a wry look. "Even one like Cornelius Lezat. He may not be the most admirable character. God knows he hurt a lot of people when his company imploded. I'm glad I didn't have any money locked into that debacle." Alvin's pudgy face grew very serious as he went on. "But I'm his attorney, and I'm supposed to do whatever I can to help him. If Lezat were able to broker the return of this painting, it might gain him some crucial goodwill and get his sentence shortened."

He sighed. "It's not saving an innocent person from an unjust murder charge, but we can't all be Perry Mason."

Liza gave Alvin his lift. He shook his head as he looked at the mess on his fender. "I'll get that cleaned up before I return the car."

"You're going to stay in Portland tonight?"

He nodded. "Not, thankfully, in the same hotel as Mr. Tarleton."

Liza drove home deep in thought. *Well, now I've seen all the competition. As far as I can see, none of them seem to be hot on the trail.*

She sighed. *At least no hotter than I am.*

The next morning, Liza came down to the kitchen ravenous—and realized there was absolutely nothing for breakfast. As she fed Rusty, she poked experimentally at his dry food and then turned away, muttering, "Yuck."

She headed downtown to Ma's Café. The breakfast crowd was just thinning out. Liza glanced around, spotting Ted Everard in one booth. As she walked over in response to his beckoning, she also saw Howard Frost rising from his seat in another booth. When he saw where she was heading, he sank back down, leaning over his empty plate and coffee.

"He looks as if he's afraid someone will sneak over and spit in his cup," Liza told Everard as she sat across from him.

"Please." Everard ran a hand over his face and looked at her with tired, red-rimmed eyes. "He was just over here, going on and on about how he hoped that with the murder inquiry cleaned up, he could expect what he called 'cooperation from the legal authorities' for his recovery efforts."

"You don't sound very cooperative," Liza said.

"I'm not feeling much like that, either," Everard replied. "I keep thinking about that note you gave me, how Dalen wished he could help his sister. Then I have to listen to that insurance company guy passing gas over how much his company had to pay out."

"Especially after they lowballed Mrs. H. on how much they had to pay out for her," Liza stopped. "This is a side of you I haven't seen before."

He looked up from reaching for his coffee cup. "What's that supposed to mean?"

"I thought records and statistics were your big thing. A sort of corporate outlook, I guess. But you're showing an interesting subversive streak."

He shrugged. "My dad wanted me to be an accountant; I wanted to be a cop. The last thing I expected to end up doing was cop accounting."

"How'd that happen?" Liza asked.

"I got shot up pretty badly two months before I was supposed to get married." Everard's words came out in a gruff tone.

He caught Liza looking at his finger. "No ring. My fiancée hung with me through some pretty rough times at the hospital, but she was out of the scene before I was finished with rehab." He sighed. "I can't really blame her. She got to thinking what it would be like, worrying about the same thing every time I went to work."

Everard looked her in the eyes with an ironic smile. "And what happens is that they give me a promotion and leave me driving a desk. This is the first time I've been out in the field in years. I don't think Clements can keep me here much longer, though. The head office will want me back on spreadsheet patrol, now that the case is supposedly solved."

Liza looked at him. "You don't sound convinced."

He frowned. "Tanino is not what you'd call a criminal genius, and Bert Clements is a good interrogator. But Vinnie Tanlines is still insisting he's innocent. They took samples off his hands and clothes to test for GSR—gunshot residue. He's acting as if he thinks this will clear him. I mean, the guy leaves a fingerprint at a murder scene, for God sakes. I don't see him outwitting us."

Liz Sanders came over to take Liza's order. She went for a heavy breakfast—fried eggs over easy, bacon, rye toast, and coffee. Everard had a rather satirical look in his eyes as he said, "And you were the one who roasted the sheriff about clogging his arteries."

"I didn't have anything to eat last night," she said indignantly. "Actually, I was offered some nice Italian food—with a red sauce." Even as she spoke, Liza moved the catsup bottle to the rear of the condiments tray.

"I'd think you'd have learned by now that murder scenes aren't pleasant places to be." A trace of last night's aggravation showed in Everard's eyes.

"I only meant to drive past. But then I saw my friend Alvin there."

"Right," Everard mocked. "Poor, helpless Alvin. You had to run and save him."

"Well, he was wearing a nice coat, and I didn't want him puking on it," she said, trying to defend herself.

That brought a twinkle of laughter to his eyes, which was replaced by a considering look. "You still looking for that painting?"

"I'm trying to help Mrs. H." Liza looked warily at the state police detective. "Why?"

"When Dalen died, I ran a search for any prison associates he might have had. One record looked interesting—a guy doing five to seven for stealing some Native American artworks. Anyway, he got out of Coastal Correctional about five years ago. I did a quick telephone interview with him, and he had nothing useful for us—not exactly surprising when an ex-con talks with the cops."

"But?" Liza said.

"But," Everard repeated, "if a non-cop talked with him, maybe he might open up a bit."

Liza's food arrived, and she attacked it with abandon. "So where would I find this ex-con art thief?" she asked with her mouth half full.

"Oh, he's not a thief anymore." That amused glint was back in Everard's eyes. "He's a security consultant, showing museums and galleries how not to get ripped off. The guy's name is Matt Augustine."

Everard consulted his notebook, then ripped out a blank page and wrote an address down. "He's got an office in downtown Portland."

15

The address Ted Everard gave Liza was actually in a neighborhood just north of Portland's downtown, a place called the Pearl. Back when Liza left Maiden's Bay for college, this area had been called "the warehouse district," a grimy industrial area.

Since then, however, artists had infiltrated, creating studios and galleries in the old manufacturing and storage buildings. Art had been the pearl hidden behind the grungy, oysterlike surroundings. That image had named the whole area.

Nowadays, high-rise condos were sprouting in what was now a hot part of town, and some of the original settlers found themselves being priced out of the neighborhood they'd created.

If Matt Augustine can afford to have an office here, he must be doing well at the security business, Liza thought. She turned onto a side street north of Burnside. The address she was looking for turned out to be a squat redbrick structure that had probably begun life as some sort of manufacturing storehouse. Now it had been renovated into living space.

Liza found Augustine's name on the downstairs buzzer board and hit the appropriate button. She breathed a silent sigh of relief when a voice answered. Although Portland was a fairly stiff drive from Maiden's Bay, she hadn't called ahead. She hadn't wanted to give Matt Augustine a chance not to see her.

"I'm hoping you can help a friend of mine with a problem," she called into the grille.

After a moment, Augustine buzzed her up.

Liza emerged from the elevator into a large, airy loft space that apparently took up an entire floor of the building. *Apparently, business must be* very *good,* she thought.

Matt Augustine was maybe five years older than Liza, but he had the face of a lively teenager, complete with close-cropped sandy hair, a small, upturned nose, and a cheerful grin that showed lots of white teeth.

His body wasn't bad either—a compact, muscular frame in a charcoal gray cable-knit turtleneck and black jeans. As he walked forward to shake hands, Liza had a strange feeling of déjà vu. Then she realized what it was. Matt Augustine moved exactly the same way Chris Dalen had.

One of Augustine's sandy eyebrows quirked. "You say you have a friend with a problem, Ms. . . . ?"

"Liza Kelly," she introduced herself. "I'm the person who found Chris Dalen's body."

Augustine removed his hand, his face shutting down. "I don't know how many ex-cons you've dealt with, Ms. Kelly. But I can give you one useful generalization. We don't like to be played."

He stepped back to rest his hip against a desk situated in front of a window that gave a wide urban landscape. "I've gotten several calls from people trying to pump my brains for clues about where Dalen hid his famous Mondrian. Hell, if I had a clue, don't you think I'd be out trying to score the reward?"

Liza gestured around. "It doesn't look as if you're doing too badly."

Augustine laughed. "As it happens, I bought into this property well before the neighborhood enjoyed its upturn."

"You mean this was a hideout in your bad old days?" Liza teased.

The former art thief tilted his head. "Not exactly. It was more like . . . a storage area to let hot items cool off."

Well, it looks as if he's cooled down a little. She reached into her bag to get out the copy of Chris Dalen's note and held it out. "I am here to help a friend. My next-door neighbor is Chris Dalen's sister."

Matt Augustine read it over. "It's the same old chicken-scratch Chris always wrote." His eyes went from the note to Liza. "Either the suits at Western Assurance Group have gotten very smart—and started hiring better-looking investigators—or you're for real."

"I taught a course at the prison, and Chris was one of my students," Liza began. She took the story through to the murder of Rod Carlowe.

Augustine shook his head. "Both Chris and I have been in worse hellholes than Coastal Correctional. But for him to waste all those years . . ."

He shrugged. "Then again, Chris could be a very stubborn guy. All he had to hear was that a job was impossible to make him bust his hump trying to pull it off. That's what got him caught over the Mondrian, you know. He had a guy on the inside—a guard—who was hinky. Anybody else would have pulled the plug. But Chris bulled ahead, the guard sang like a canary at the first question from the cops, and Chris got nailed."

"But not before he stashed the painting." Liza looked at Augustine. "You must have gotten on with him very well for him to tell you so much. Except for kidding around, he was pretty close-mouthed around me."

"I knew him before he wound up in the joint," Augustine admitted. "Often in our business, you wind up serving a sort of apprenticeship to learn the trade. That's what I did with Chris."

He laughed. "And as a kid, Chris did the same thing with a guy named Otto. Half of the lessons he'd do just the way Otto told him, in this terrible accent. I guess Otto was great with locks, but English was definitely a second language for him. 'Mitt der English, not zo goot,' Chris would say."

Liza joined in. "You sounded exactly like him. 'Zum-day, I call you on der telefunken.' "

Augustine threw his head back, cracking up. "Oh, yeah, 'Telefunken!' I guess poor old Otto never quite got the hang of 'telephone.' " He actually had to wipe his eyes at that memory. But when he looked at Liza again, Matt Augustine had an odd expression on his face.

"Everybody else who asked me, I told them I hadn't been in touch with Chris since I left the joint. Being on parole, you're not supposed to associate with known felons." He glanced over at the collection of items on his desk. "That wasn't exactly true. I had a visit from a guy who got out a few weeks ago—a guy with a message from Chris."

Liza stared. "What did he want?"

"Believe it or not, a telephone. One of those cheapo, throwaway cell phones. I had to figure out how to get the number to him, and arrange for it to be waiting in one of our old pickups—"

"Like Patrician Books?" Liza asked.

Augustine looked a little surprised, but then he shook his head. "No, Patrick was just for messages. We had other places for leaving tools, or . . . merchandise."

He gestured out the window at the cityscape. "Of course, with so many renovations going on all over the place, a lot of our old drop points have disappeared. But I found one, and I left der telefunken in it. Thought I'd get a call from Chris after he got out, maybe even see him again." He raised his shoulders, then let them slump. "Instead—"

"Bad things happened," Liza said. She picked up Chris Dalen's note. "He said it was possible here. But when he asked for my help, he seemed to think I shouldn't have any problem finding the Mondrian. Is there something here that I'm missing?"

Matt Augustine took another long, hard look at the photocopy. Then he shook his head. "Not that I can see."

The afternoon shadows kept getting longer as Liza drove back home to Maiden's Bay—not that she much noticed, though. All the way, she kept going over her conversation with Matt Augustine, squaring what he'd said about Chris Dalen with what she knew of the man. Some points matched up—the weird sense of humor, his fractured sauerkraut accent . . . his stubbornness.

But his obvious camaraderie with his student and colleague, that was a surprise. Chris Dalen had always struck her as an island, in solitary even in the midst of the prison population.

He must have missed Matt after he got parole, Liza thought. Then she shook her head. *I might have heard a lot about Chris Dalen the human being, but I got no further figuring him out as a code maker.* Sighing, she took the exit for Maiden's Bay and drove through town.

When she got home to Hackleberry Avenue, Liza quite disappointed Rusty by pretty much walking past his capering welcome. Instead, she plumped herself down at her improvised desk in the living room, spreading out the two sheets of paper Chris Dalen had sent in front of her.

What a difference, she thought, looking from one to the other. The photocopy of Dalen's note was wildly scrawled. But the miniature reproduction of the Mondrian was carefully, even lovingly, crafted, the lines as precisely drawn as if this were a drafting blueprint, the colors, even in the photocopy applied evenly, not daubed or blotched. There was even a little "T" written by the upper left and an equally small "B" at the lower right. Chris had wanted to make sure this version of the Mondrian avoided the ignominy of hanging upside down like the original.

The note gave every suggestion of something created at the very last minute. But the picture must have been done some time well in advance.

"So what does that tell me?" Liza muttered, frowning at the enigmatic pair of clues.

Feeling left out, Rusty crept over and gently insinuated his muzzle between Liza's right arm and her ribs. Then he shook his head vigorously, jerking her arm aside. Startled, Liza looked down. "Sorry for ignoring you, big guy."

She reached down to scratch his head, then squinted at a crumpled piece of paper on the floor. It was the sudoku puzzle that Chris had created for her course—a piece of paper that should have been on her workspace.

"Rusty!" Liza's voice grew stern. "Have you been jumping up on the table again?"

The dog's head immediately slipped from under her hand as he began slinking away.

"Bad dog!" Liza called after him. She got out of the chair and knelt to retrieve the puzzle. The solution had fallen farther under the table, but further searching failed to turn up any other papers that might have been knocked down. Reaching up blindly, she stuck the puzzle and solution on the tabletop.

"Nothing else," she said, "unless a big, dopey dog carried it away." She glared after Rusty, who sped up his slinking off to a scurry. Liza crawled out from under the table and got back in her chair. The paper she had tossed up half-covered Chris Dalen's posthumous communications.

"Hunh?" Liza said as she went to remove the puzzle from over the picture. "They're almost the same size . . ."

Her gaze fell on the note. The top of the page was covered by Dalen's puzzle solution, but she could see the last sentence. **If you can put this over . . .**

Her IM discussion with Uncle Jim had talked about code overlays. Maybe she'd just been laying them over the wrong message. The translucent Mondrian wasn't supposed to go over Chris Dalen's note. It was supposed to overlay the puzzle.

But what was she supposed to see? Liza pulled out he note and read the first line: **Maybe I'm just in a blue funk.** The title of the stolen Mondrian was *Composition in Blue, Red, and Green.*

And Dalen continually gave the telephone the joking name of "der telefunken."

Liza abruptly turned to her computer and began running Google to find color images of *Composition in Blue, Red, and Green.* Once she got that, Liza started comparing the image on her computer monitor with the photocopy in her hand, trying to see which of the spaces were blue, green, and red. The red areas were pretty easy to distinguish— they appeared almost black on the photocopy.

The blues and greens came out in shades of gray, and that's where Liza had to be careful telling one from the other.

Once she got the colored areas correctly marked, she set the Mondrian copy over Dalen's sudoku and held it up to the light from her monitor. It wasn't as clear as it would have been with the translucent paper, but she could see numbers showing up in the blue sections.

However, there were very few numbers at all in the seventeen-clue puzzle.

Liza aligned the puzzle solution with the mini-Mondrian. Then she grabbed a pencil and began scribbling down all the numbers she found in blue-colored areas.

She wound up with ten digits. The first three were 9, 7, and 1. Her breath came a little faster. That was an area code used around Portland.

The rest of the digits weren't so familiar: 5, 5, 5, 4, 3, 9, and 4.

"No, I don't recognize it," Liza murmured. "But it could be a phone number."

She sat for a long moment, staring at the sequence of numbers. Then, taking a deep breath, she picked up the handset of her phone and began tapping the numbers into the keypad with a trembling finger.

"I'm gonna feel pretty stupid if I end up getting a Chinese restaurant in Beaverton," she told Rusty over her shoulder. "For one thing, I don't think they'll deliver this far out of town."

The number connected, and Liza heard the bleep of a phone ringing on the other end of the line. One, two . . . it kept up for five rings, and then voice mail came on.

"Hello there," a voice said.

Liza gasped as she recognized Chris Dalen speaking.

"Looks like you've figured things out to get this far. All I can say is go ahead. Everything should be a go."

PART FOUR:
Not-So-Simple Endings

One of the comforting things about sudoku is that after beating your brains out on the most difficult puzzle, the end of a solution brings you back to the most simple techniques. Rows and columns will be filled in except for one measly space, so it's just a case of turning off your brain and filling things in, right?

Actually, this is the point where you can get distracted and suddenly find a space that holds *no* candidates, completely invalidating your solution.

As the great Yogi Berra put it, "It ain't over till it's over." So pay attention and try to avoid any unpleasant last-minute surprises.

—Excerpt from *Sudo-cues* by Liza K

16

As the dead man's voice died away, Liza's mood quickly shifted from awe to aggravation. She wasn't about to leave a message. Instead, she set the receiver down with a bang and let rip with a few choice words until Rusty began to bark.

She glanced guiltily over at her dog. "Yes," she told him defensively, "I know those words. Sorry to offend your virgin ears." Then she shook her head at her own foolishness. No doubt Rusty was reacting more to her tone of voice than to her vocabulary.

As she patted the dog to calm him down, her eyes went back to the telephone. She'd made a breakthrough, figuring out some of Chris Dalen's thought processes. But he definitely had the kind of mind that would fit around a corkscrew. Obviously, there were some more twists and turns to negotiate before she had the full message.

Liza turned to the telephone again and began dialing. Her first call was next door to Mrs. Halvorsen's for Michael. Then her fingers hovered in hesitation over the keypad, suddenly reluctant to enter the number for the Killamook Inn.

She shook her head. Yes, she was disappointed with Kevin, even a little angry. But there was the case to consider. He had helped in the past. Turning to him now would also give him the chance to make up for what he'd done.

Biting her lip, Liza called the inn. Kevin promised to set off immediately.

The next number caused her a shorter hesitation, a bare moment before she punched in the number for the sheriff's substation down at City Hall.

She was in luck—Ted Everard was back in Sheriff Clements's office. "This may be a dirty word to you," Liza said into the phone, "but I found a clue. I'm having some people over to discuss it, and I'd like you to be here, too."

"A clue," he repeated. "Does this have anything to do with our conversation earlier today?"

"You might say that," Liza replied.

"Anything else?" Everard pressed.

Liza suddenly thought of the empty state of her kitchen shelves. "Well, you could bring snacks."

While she waited for them all to arrive, Liza managed to find some tracing paper and redid the Mondrian overlay, this time in color.

They convened over sodas, pretzels, and chips that the state police investigator had brought. Liza quickly took them through her conversation with Matt Augustine.

Everard quickly interrupted. "He had a cell phone? It wasn't found with him or in his room." He looked at Liza. "Remember his personal effects? Either Augustine was spinning you a story, or whoever killed Dalen took the phone."

"Augustine wasn't telling fairy tales," Liza said. She went through her own process of discovery, realizing that the Mondrian reproduction matched the puzzle Dalen had given her at the final sudoku class, the blue funk—telefunken connection, the ten digits she'd gotten. Then she dialed the number, putting her phone on speaker.

The four of them listened to Chris Dalen's greeting.

When it was over, Liza hung up. Kevin shook his head. " 'Go ahead,' he said. But go where?"

"Could it be to go ahead with the puzzle?" Everard suggested. "Take away that phone number and you have—"

He went to count, but Liza headed him off. "Seventy-one spaces remaining."

"Most of them are white," Michael said. "Is that where we should go first?"

"There are three colors left," Kevin pointed out. "Maybe there are three more sets of information that we need."

"Or three sentences, if this is some kind of code." Everard stared so hard at the puzzle, Liza began to worry he was about to burn a hole through it.

"Maybe we're getting too fancy with this," Michael suggested. "Dalen obviously had to be tricky, but I think he also had to follow the KISS principle."

"Kiss?" Kevin gave him an uncomprehending look.

"Keep It Simple, Stupid," Michael replied with a beatific smile.

Everard managed to get hold of Kevin's arm before he slugged Michael. "It's an acronym," he said. "K-I-S-S."

"So how do *you* 'Keep It Simple, Stupid'?" Kevin angrily asked Michael.

Michael shrugged. "Blue was for telephone. What color is for go?"

All eyes went to him as they said almost in unison, "Green!"

Consulting the puzzle and the overlay, they ended up with fifteen digits.

Everard frowned at the little line of numbers. "So what good does this do us?" He tapped the blue squares. "Blue meant a telephone number that was supposed to be called. If green means go, then these numbers should represent somewhere—"

"Where we should go," Michael chimed in.

"So what is it?" Everard asked. "An address? There are

numbered avenues in Portland, but I don't think you end up with fifteen digits."

"Maybe they threw in the zip code," Michael said. "Or the zip plus four."

"Portland zip codes begin with a ninety-seven," Everard told him.

Kevin tapped one of the red areas on the overlay. "You know, red is the color usually connected with hell."

Michael's head snapped his way. "So?"

"Well, it's another place you could go," Kevin replied with a shrug.

"And what's that supposed to mean?" Michael demanded.

Kevin shrugged again. "Just an observation."

"Maybe you should keep your brilliant observations to yourself," Michael said.

"I'd be glad to—if you could do the same," Kevin shot back.

Liza rolled her eyes. So what's the next line going to be? she wondered, *"Make me" or "Bite me"?*

Everard took advantage of the bickering to lean closer on the couch with Liza. "Hope you didn't invite me here hoping to recruit a Curly so you could take this Stooges act on the road."

"Actually," Liza told him, her voice a little sour, "I had you more pegged as a Moe."

That would have gotten a laugh out of him, except that the volume—and the bad blood—between Kevin and Michael kept escalating.

"You better back down, Langley." Kevin was out of his seat now, looming over Michael, his hands clenched into fists. "Keep running your mouth like that, and someone's going to shut it for you."

Michael bounced right out of his chair to stand nose to nose with Kevin. "Nobody in my family ever backed off from a bully, Shepard. Our family motto is 'Fifty-four forty or fight!'"

Ted Everard got to his feet and with two quick motions, separated the two. Liza saw that he didn't actually get between them, but had stationed himself to restrain either one of them from going at the other.

"Actually, Langley, our side did back down in that argument," he pointed out in a calm voice. "Way down. President Polk and the Brits signed a treaty setting most of the border between the U.S. and Canada along the forty-eighth parallel of latitude—"

He broke off, risking a quick glance at Liza while still standing ready to keep Michael and Kevin from tangling. "Liza, read the first few numbers that we just wrote down."

"Four, five, six, seven . . . ," she began.

"Should that tell us something?" Michael snapped.

"Considering that the international border is several hundred miles north of us, it might mean something to a guide who's up on all the latest bells and whistles." Everard looked at Kevin, who suddenly put down his hands and stepped back, slipping out of fighting mode.

"You're right. I should have seen it." He spoke with a healthy tone of self-disgust in his voice. "I've even done some GPS-guided hiking."

Michael looked from Kevin to Ted Everard to Liza, his own aggression melting away in confusion. "I still don't—"

"The city of Portland stands at forty-five degrees north latitude," Everard said.

The lightbulb went on over Michael's head. "And the magic numbers we just found start with four and five." He frowned. "But there are an awful lot of numbers after that."

"GPS devices go out to five decimal places on a degree of latitude or longitude, getting as detailed a plot as possible." Kevin went to the coffee table to look at their number set again. "That means the latitude would be seven digits long, and the next three digits—" He put his finger on the paper. "Yup, they're one, two, and four. That's our local longitude. Actually, we're closer to 125 degrees west, but around here that's out in the Pacific Ocean."

"So we've got a location." Excitement filled Michael's voice as he forgot the near-brawl completely. "We've got a place to go."

"We know where the painting is!" Kevin was equally psyched.

Everard poured some cold water on their enthusiasm. "Unless we get there and find a coffee can with another puzzle in it."

"Bite your tongue," Liza told him. She wasn't going to whoop and holler like her two beaus, but she was pretty eager, too.

"I've got a GPS tracker," Kevin announced. "It's too dark to try it now, but we can go out tomorrow morning and find this sucker."

"This requires something a little more serious in the celebration department than soda and chips," Michael said. "Suppose we take this part to that place out of town—the Famished Farmer. The food is decent, and so are the drinks."

Liza looked at him in surprise. The Famished Farmer was also the site of one of their more recent escapades. She and Ava Barnes had left Michael with a table full of drinks, the bill, and, in the eyes of the wait staff, the bag, while making an unorthodox exit to escape the possibility of being tailed. *Choosing there of all places—that's a bit unexpected,* she thought.

Then again, maybe it wasn't so unexpected. Maiden's Bay wasn't exactly the home of diversified dining. Ma's Café took care of most of the high-cholesterol food. Fruit of the Sea was the fancy-schmantzy place in town, but a bit too buttoned-down for a celebration. There were a couple of taverns that served greasy burgers with a side order of bar brawl . . . of course, there was the dining room at the Killamook Inn, but Michael didn't want to give Kevin the advantage of fighting on his home ground.

"Okay, the Famished Farmer it is," she said, going to get her coat.

"You can come in my SUV," Kevin offered.

"Or in my car," Everard said.

Liza shook her head and held up her keys. "Michelle Markson's first rule of parties—always make sure you can get home on your own."

She led the way, with Michael navigating from the passenger's seat. The restaurant had gone up on the outskirts of town and was fairly new. It was part of a chain, complete with a rural theme. The place had been done up to look like a barn, and she could spot the logo more than a mile away—a neon farmer with a knife and fork in each hand, with a big red tongue flicking back and forth.

Michael laughed. "It's hard to imagine, but that looks even more grotesque in the dark."

Still, they found a good number of cars in the parking lot. Inside, the farm motif continued, with lots of hand-aged unfinished wood and straw bales for patrons to sit on while waiting for tables. At this time of evening they got right in. A waitress in jeans and a plaid shirt led them to a booth that looked very much like a cow stall.

"Very elegant." Kevin couldn't keep the sneer from his voice as he slid in.

"Yeah, well, try the steak and not the veal—that's what the waitress told me last time I was here."

They ordered a round of beers, and Liza examined a menu with the size and heft of a world atlas. Apparently the cuisine at the Famished Farmer involved food and more food.

She put the tome down and looked around. Frankly, this Disneyland version of down-home seemed oppressive to her. That subversive corner of her mind threw out an odd thought. *This is the kind of ambience that drove Chris Dalen off to become a crook.*

Liza looked at the details—those impressive-looking rough-hewn beams actually looked pretty old. Maybe they had been cannibalized from a real barn to add an air of authenticity to this joint.

Lot of barns being knocked down in the name of progress, she thought. *Not to mention farmhouses like the one where Mrs. H. grew up.*

Just when she thought she couldn't feel more out of place, she spotted an even more incongruous figure. Apparently Howard Frost was feeling a chill, because he hadn't taken off that dreadful brown polyester parka. He was sitting at a table for one, isolated off to the side. Liza wasn't sure whether he was just bent forward over his plate or huddled there.

As she gazed at him, Frost glanced up and their eyes met. For a second, Liza thought he was going to come over—he'd pretty much pressed each opportunity before. Instead, the insurance investigator looked back down at his plate and reached for the drink at his elbow.

Liza was going to point him out to Everard, but that's when their beers arrived. True to the Famished Farmer philosophy, the steins were ridiculously oversized.

"I've bought pitchers that were smaller than this," Michael said, hefting his drink.

"Probably at some wimpy Hollywood place where they don't really drink beer, they just go to the little boys' room and get high." Kevin's words might have been heavy-handed teasing, except for the undercurrent of challenge in his tone.

"You think I can't hold my beer?" Michael asked mildly, and then drained half of Frankenstein's stein. "Growing up in my hometown, all we had was beer and fishing. And I didn't like going out for the fishing."

"Yeah, but did you like the beer?" Kevin chugged the contents of his stein and set it down with a bang. "I'm sorry, Detective, maybe we shouldn't be doing this around you."

"Me?" Everard raised his stein for a hearty swig. He hadn't announced it, but Liza noticed he'd already lowered the beer level by half. "Don't you guys watch the police shows on TV? About half the action takes place in cop bars."

The waitress returned, and the guys went for another round of drinks, followed by food orders. Liza was still working her way through the first monster tankard when huge platters of food arrived.

"Awesome!" said Everard, going to work on a steak with a fork and what looked like a serrated Bowie knife.

Excessive, was how the voice in Liza's head described the celebratory feast. The portion sizes were ridiculous. Mutant baked potatoes slathered with sour cream, a mound of several kinds of squash and beans that had been over-cooked, a loaf of sourdough bread bigger than her head with a lump of half-frozen butter as large as her fist. The meat was good, but it looked as if it had come off a mammoth rather than a cow.

She ended up taking a doggy bag that bulged grotesquely—and that was just the remains of the steak. If she used this as a garnish for his regular food, Rusty would be eating like a king for the next week.

Liza pushed away her still unfinished stein. No one else in the booth wanted coffee, and she wasn't sure what round of beer the boys were on, but enough had been consumed to pretty much kill table conversation unless she wanted to beat on her chest. She also turned down the house dessert, something called Chocolate Overindulgence that involved chocolate layer cake, a brownie, brandy, hot fudge, and whipped cream. The waitress tried for a lyrical description, but it just brought a shudder to Liza's overfull stomach.

"Look, guys, about tomorrow morning—" she began.

"We'll give you a call." Michael pointed at Kevin. "*You* should give her a call, since you got the dingus."

He slurred a little, turning the last word into something more like "dingish."

Kevin nodded heavily. "Yeah. Yeah. I'll do that. You don't have to worry. Yeah."

Everard kept his mouth shut but rolled his eyes.

"I'll call it a night then," Liza said. "I'll wait for your call."

She rose, and the guys got out of their seats.

"I'll leave a twenty for my part of the bill—"

"Nah, nah," Everard said. "It's on us." His elocution wasn't crisp, but he didn't sound as bad off as the other two.

"What say we take this party to the bar?" Michael suggested.

Outside, Liza took a deep breath of chilly air, clearing her head. *First time I ever had a contact high on beer,* she thought as she got into her car. It was a quick drive home.

Rusty sniffed very interestedly at the bag in her hand as Liza came through the door. "Tomorrow," she told him sternly as she stowed it in the refrigerator. Then she went upstairs, brushed her teeth, undressed, and fell into bed.

She woke in total darkness, feeling vaguely sick and headachy. But that wasn't what had roused her. The phone rang again, that obnoxious bleating noise ramming a spike through each ear and into the middle of her brain.

Liza fumbled the handset into place. "H'lo?" It came out way too breathy.

The voice on the other end of the line was a harsh whisper—a slap in the face from an ice-cold hand. "You may have found the painting, bitch, but I've got the old woman."

17

Sitting up in the darkness, Liza listened to that harsh, cold, whispering voice. It was like being in a nightmare, with the added horror of being awake.

It wasn't a conversation, or even a discussion, more like a harangue. "I'll call again in two hours. You'd better be ready to deal. It's probably too much to ask you to keep the police out of this. Just tell your friend the sheriff and that stumblebum state policeman this—the first cop car I see will get to see me blowing your neighbor's brains out."

The phone clicked off, and Liza leapt from the bed, tearing around her room to get dressed. She clattered down the stairs, waking Rusty, who gave an interrogative sort of bark.

Liza paid no attention, throwing open the door, slamming it behind her, and slopping through the snow to Mrs. Halvorsen's house. If Mrs. H. had disappeared, wouldn't Michael have noticed? Why hadn't he called or come over?

She went to knock, and the door gave back from her fist.

Open? The discovery chilled Liza worse than the cold, dark air around her. *The door is open?*

She pushed her way into the house to find one dim lamp on. The little knickknack table at the entrance to the living room lay on its side, amid a couple of smashed figurines. Then she saw the two larger figures—one sprawled on the couch, the other on the floor.

"Ohmigod!" It came out almost as a hum because she had gritted her teeth to keep any screams from coming out. Liza was getting very, very tired of finding dead bodies. She felt she was definitely over her quota for this year—and perhaps for the next five.

Liza dropped to her knees beside the body on the floor. It was facedown, and she held her breath as she turned it over.

"Michael!" she sobbed, pulling his lifeless form to her.

The body gave a great snort of a snore and then expelled a blast of beer-breath in her face.

"Michael!" Liza wasn't sobbing now—she was hopping mad. "Wake up!" She shook him.

He grunted.

"Goddammit, Michael!" Liza smacked him on one cheek, then the other. Finally, she hauled off and gave him a good shot.

"Hunh?" Michael's eyes fluttered open, and he put a hand to his cheek. "Ow!"

Liza waved away more beer fumes. "Where's Mrs. Halvorsen?"

That brought a couple of confused blinks from him. "Uh . . . upstairs?" She let go of him, and his head landed on the floor with a thump.

Another "Ow!" rose behind her as she flew up the stairs. The doorway to the master bedroom was open, but Mrs. H. wasn't there.

She had been—the bed was unmade, several drawers hung open, and a couple of mismatched shoes stood in front of the open closet door. Mrs. H. would never have left the place looking like this.

Not willingly, Liza thought. Her brain was half frozen with fear and half burning with anger. She stomped back downstairs, discovering as she did that the living room was much colder than upstairs.

The open door, she thought. Then she realized it was more than that. The slit she had repaired in the protective plastic was open again—torn open, by the looks of it.

Liza glared down at Michael, who was attempting to pull himself off the floor by climbing onto the couch. So far, all he'd succeeded in doing was reviving the other sodden form, Kevin Shepard. He'd grumble unintelligibly and shift, and, since Michael was trying to use Kevin's knees as a brace, that would send Michael back to the floor again.

"Wake up!" Liza shouted. "Wake up, the both of you!" Her voice got louder. "Mrs. H. got kidnapped while you two were sleeping it off!" That got through to them. Kevin and Michael slowly fumbled their way to their feet until they stood in front of the couch, swaying slightly. They made a pretty sad pair, blinking owlishly at Liza while struggling to keep their balance.

"What happened?" Liza demanded.

"Nuh—nothing," Kevin rasped, then stopped to clear his throat.

"Somebody brought us here—I kinda remember that," Michael amplified. "I helped Kevin in—"

"No, I helped *you* in," Kevin suddenly said. "You hit the table."

"Oh?" Michael looked ready to argue with Kevin until his eye fell on the upended table and its shattered contents. "Oh-oh."

"That must have made some crash," Liza said. "And Mrs. H. didn't come down?"

Michael shook his head, trying to look virtuous. "We thought she was asleep."

"Yeah," Kevin echoed. "It was after midnight."

"You weren't thinking of her at all," Liza accused. "The two of you just took a few more steps and flopped on your faces." She paused for a second. If Mrs. Halvorsen had been

around, the drunken banging and crashing would certainly
have brought her down.

That means she must have been gone before the guys
got back, Liza realized. So the bad guy hadn't just waltzed
past their sodden forms. On the other hand, if Michael had
actually made it upstairs in a condition to notice things,
they'd have known about the abduction hours ago.

She stabbed both index fingers at them. "You two—
upstairs—cold showers. I'm going to the kitchen to make
some coffee. Lots of coffee."

Mrs. H. was a tea drinker, but she kept a jar of instant
coffee for guests. Liza made two cups, black, and strong
enough for the spoon to stand up in the middle of the
cup.

Michael came down first, his clothes fresh, his hair still
damp, moving as if he feared someone had been tinkering
with his body joints and not put them back together prop-
erly. He sat in silence as Liza pushed a cup of coffee toward him.

Then she turned to the telephone and called the police.
"This is Liza Kelly. I'm at 37 Hackleberry Avenue," she
said, giving Mrs. Halvorsen's address. "I got a phone call
saying my neighbor had been kidnapped, and when I came
over, she wasn't here."

"We'll get a patrol car over there right away, and I'm
sure the sheriff will be heading over from Killamook," the
duty deputy said.

Liza hesitated, then said, "I suppose you should also get
in touch with Detective Everard—"

"He's here in the back, ma'am. Hold on."

A second later, Ted Everard's voice came over the line,
crisp and businesslike. "Everard here."

"Well, it doesn't sound as if they woke you up. How do
you do that?"

"Let's just say our little competition last night turned
out to be a pro-am sport." He didn't have to mention who

the amateurs were. "I made sure your friends got home safely, made a couple of preparations for myself, and then slept over here."

In a cell, she finished for him.

"I had a change of clothes on hand—that's what happens when you live out of a suitcase. Anyway, I got up at my usual time, and here I am."

As he spoke, Kevin shuffled his way into the kitchen and sat beside Michael. The two of them looked like half-drowned kittens—the runts of the litter that old-line farmers would have stuck in a bag and tossed in the river. Obviously, the shock to their systems had pushed them from half-drunk to full hangover mode.

"So what's this I hear about your neighbor?" Everard asked.

Liza told him what had happened, ending with a glance at her watch. "Oh, God, he'll be calling back in little more than an hour."

"Okay, then," Ted said. "I'll have to roust some telephone people out of bed so we have a shot at tracing that call. See you at your house ASAP."

"He said—" Liza began, but Everard finished for her.

"Don't involve the cops, right?"

"No. He just said for you and Sheriff Clements to stay out of the way."

"We'll just have to see about that," Ted replied. "See you soon."

After the first deputies arrived, Liza, Michael, and Kevin went to her house. Soon enough, Sheriff Clements and Ted Everard joined them as well as several phone company technicians, who hooked up an extra extension and spliced in their tracing equipment.

Liza's brain had finally unfrozen, leaving her with lots of questions.

"I don't understand how this guy knew we'd figured out the location of the painting," she said to the sheriff.

"Yes, especially since *I* didn't know about it, either," Clements said, directing a black look toward Ted Everard.

"We didn't know for sure we had found the picture," Ted replied to the sheriff. "That's why we were going to check it out this morning."

To Liza he said, "As for the kidnapper finding out, it wouldn't be so hard to do—provided he had Chris Dalen's cell phone."

"Dalen had a cell phone?" Clements asked.

"That's what Liza found out yesterday," Everard told the sheriff. "It wasn't found among his effects."

"Which means that this kidnapper also killed Dalen," Clements said.

Everard nodded. "And if he had the phone, he probably heard Chris Dalen's outgoing voice message. The one that congratulated the caller on figuring things out—"

"But it didn't give a usable clue as to where the Mondrian was hidden," Liza finished. "Not unless you had all the other clues."

"However, the killer could keep tracking any incoming messages, knowing that whoever called must have cracked the code," Everard went on.

"Then all he'd need to do was check into the incoming number to find out who that was," Clements rumbled. "He could use a reverse telephone directory. Hell, nowadays some phone companies will even do that for you."

This time his black look was aimed at the phone company employees, who studiously refused to meet his eyes. They settled into a tense silence. But a very disturbing logical equation kept swirling around in Liza's head.

The killer of Chris Dalen had the dead man's cell phone.

The person who'd kidnapped Mrs. H. also apparently had that cell phone.

Therefore, Elise Halvorsen was in the hands of a killer, QED. Liza remembered that from logic class—*quod erat demonstrandum*. Translated from the Latin, that meant "what was to be proved."

Right now, she fervently hoped that QED wouldn't turn out to mean Quite Extremely Dead.

The ring from the telephone seemed considerably more shrill than usual. Certainly, it seemed to slash right through Michael and Kevin's heads. They both winced as Liza picked up the handset in unison with the sheriff and Ted Everard. In the background, she could see one of the telephone techs doing something on a laptop.

"Hello?" she said.

Instead of the kidnapper, she heard the annoyed tones of Mrs. H. "Be careful, dear, he's crazy—"

She abruptly went off the phone, and that whispering voice came on. "Do you have it?"

"No," Liza replied. "I tried to tell you that before. But we think we know where it is by latitude and longitude."

"So you need to find it by GPS," the whisperer growled. "What are the coordinates?"

Liza gave them.

"How far?"

Liza repeated the question, and Kevin looked up. The police had brought some detailed maps, and he'd been examining them. "It looks as if the plot is in the Cape Sinestra State Park up along the coast. Maybe half an hour to forty-five minutes, but it may take longer getting through the park to the spot itself."

Liza relayed this information. The whisperer on the other side of the line was silent for a couple of seconds.

When he spoke again, his voice was harsher than ever. "You've got an hour. One car. Bring a couple of your friends to help dig—if they're capable. And no cops. You hear that, Sheriff?"

Clements stood stone-faced with the receiver up to his ear. He didn't break his silence.

"I know you have to be on the line. So you heard that the old broad is all right—at least so far. But if I see one cop car—marked or unmarked—she's gonna be history."

18

No sooner did the kidnapper cut the connection than Sheriff Clements whirled on the telephone people. "Well?"

"It's a cell phone." One of the technicians consulted one of his pieces of equipment. "We got the number—it's 971-555-4394."

Liza double-checked the string of "blue numbers" she had written down. "That's the number of the phone that Chris Dalen had."

"Waste not, want not," Ted Everard said. "The kidnapper's got it, and it comes in handy to hide his identity."

The sheriff went over to the telephone guy on the laptop. "Most important—did you locate where the call came from?"

The computer operator shrugged. "It was barely a minute. We just got it traced to the nearest cell tower. I can tell you the call was made somewhere in the northern end of town."

"That doesn't do much to zero in on the kidnapper," Clements complained. "I mean, *we're* in the northern end of town. All you've told me is the pretty obvious fact that this clown is in Maiden's Bay."

"Well, the conversation also told us that he's from out of town," Everard said. "He needed directions to get to the exchange site."

Liza barely paid attention to this comment. She was staring worriedly at Michael and Kevin. "Are the two of you feeling well enough to go? We're kind of racing the clock here."

"Yes!" Michael all but jumped to his feet. Then he paused in embarrassment. "Except for a bad case of caffeine bladder."

He ran for the bathroom while Liza got her car keys. Sheriff Clements stepped to block the door. "I can't say I'm enthusiastic about this," he rumbled.

"If you've got an alternative plan that won't get Mrs. H. killed, I'd be happy to hear it," Liza said. "Because I'm not jumping for joy myself."

"Kidnapping is a federal matter," the sheriff said, his voice so low he was almost talking to himself. "But by the time we get to the FBI, and they get one of their agents over here from Portland, this would be all over."

He shook his head. "So, if you and your friends are willing to go . . ."

Ted Everard interrupted him, stepping forward. "I'm going, too."

Clements looked dubious. "Are you sure that's a good idea, Ted? This guy sounded pretty firm when he said no cops."

"He said no cop *cars*," Ted said, splitting hairs. "By the time he's close enough to identify me, we'll be at the point of transferring the painting. I'm willing to bet that greed will trump caution." He looked from Clements to Liza. "What do you think?"

"I think it would be a good idea to have a professional along," Liza admitted. *Especially one with a gun*, she added silently.

Sighing, Clements stepped aside. "I won't stand in your way."

"Well, come on then." Liza stepped outside into the dawn's early light, Kevin and Everard nearly bumping into her as she skidded to a stop. She'd just noticed something she hadn't seen in the darkness earlier. Kevin's black SUV stood parked in Mrs. Halvorsen's driveway.

Liza turned to Kevin, pointing at his vehicle. "If we're going to hit the trails in some state park, maybe we should take your truck." She looked at him carefully. "Are you okay for driving?"

He nodded, looking determined.

"Fine. Then you go and start 'er up." Liza ran next door to the garage, where Mrs. H. stored her gardening implements. Rummaging around, she managed to snag a heavy mattock and a shovel, throwing them into the rear of the SUV.

Then she stopped in surprise, watching Ted Everard climbing in on the driver's side. "Kevin figured it might be better if he took the navigator's seat," the state cop explained. "I brought along a GPS gizmo, but he's the one with experience in actually using one." Kevin had already established himself in the shotgun position, an electronic unit about the size of a large hardcover book in his hands.

"This thing even plots a route to the coordinates—at least as far as mapped roads will take us," he said.

Liza got in the backseat. A moment later, Michael joined them. Ted Everard had already warmed up the engine. They pulled out, threading their way through the collection of police and telephone vehicles parked helter-skelter along Hackleberry Avenue.

Following Kevin's instructions, they headed off for the 101. Soon they were on the highway headed south. It wasn't exactly the sort of ride that encouraged conversation. Finally, Liza said, "Shouldn't we be trying to come up with a plan or something?"

From behind the wheel, Everard sighed. "I think the plan is to play it straight—make the exchange—unless the kidnapper tries to pull something."

He glanced in the mirror and caught Liza's eye. "Remember that time in Clements's office where I said I didn't want to end up depending on the girl detective and her chums?"

Ted sighed again. "And here I am, depending on the girl detective and her chums."

Yeah, Liza thought. *There's a great mystery series in there*—Detective Girl and the Hangover Boys. *The thing is, we have to bring our best game to this. Mrs. H. is depending on us to get her back safely.*

"I don't know how good my 'detecting' has been," Liza finally admitted. "Can any of our suspects be the kidnapper? Tanino is still in jail, isn't he?"

Everard nodded. "He was moved over to Killamook, but he's going to get out on bail when court convenes this morning. The GSR test came back negative." His voice got a little more sour. "Either he's innocent, or he's really got us fooled with that stupid act. Of course, you never know with mob guys. One of the big bosses used to walk around his neighborhood in his bathrobe, drooling, to convince people he was crazy."

"Yeah, but there's a big difference between crazy and stupid." Liza went on down the suspect list. "Carlowe is dead, and Alvin Hunzinger is out of town." She had a hard time imagining that terrifying whispered voice coming from Alvin. "What about Fritz Tarleton?"

"He's collecting his darling daughter from Coastal Correctional this morning," Everard reported. "I think this whole exchange thing would represent a scheduling conflict."

"How about Tarleton's security chief?" Liza tried to remember his name. "MacBain, McShane? He's about the only one left."

"We could add one name to the list," Everard said. "I got word this morning that Fat Frankie Basso got out of Coastal yesterday afternoon. Apparently some friends in high places worked to expedite his departure."

"And here I thought we'd worked things out," Liza groused.

"I guess the process of elimination works better in sudoku than in murder investigating," Everard told her with a shrug. Everyone else in the car was too sunk in hangovers to argue the point.

Liza looked out the window. A lot of the Oregon coast was devoted to parkland. Right now the view was of fir trees climbing the lower reaches of the Cascade Range, the whole vista sprinkled with snow. The weather report for the day had been "partly cloudy," as it was for about 180 days a year. Clouds had been thick earlier, but now errant rays of sunshine had managed to break through, creating occasional dazzling spots on an otherwise shadowy landscape.

"The woods are lovely, dark and deep," Liza quoted to herself. And they were—no dogs running out to pee on the snow, or kids tramping through it, and except for the area near the road, no traffic grinding away some of it while belching exhaust over the rest.

Liza's mind went back to business. *But we have promises to keep. I wonder how many more miles we have before we get where we're going.*

They passed a large carved wooden sign: Cape Sinestra State Park. Kevin straightened up in his seat, watching the GPS unit like a hawk. "We're coming up on the coordinates."

A little farther along they found a low stone wall, with an opening for a gravel path. Everard braked. "Should I take the turn?" he asked Kevin.

"It's heading in the right direction," came the reply.

The SUV bounced along an increasingly sketchy trail that seemed to aim straight for the Pacific in the distance. They came out on a rocky promontory where the trail petered out . . . and where they found Mrs. Halvorsen's monster Oldsmobile.

Liza took a few steps past the old car and peered downward. A hundred feet below, waves that had traveled a couple of thousand miles across the ocean were smashing against sheer rocky walls.

"Impressive," she said.

"But kind of bare," Michael observed. "Not too many places to hide something." He peered around. "Unless there's a cave or a crevice somewhere."

"Don't knock yourself out looking yet. We still have a little way to go," Kevin told them.

Everard sighed again. "Let's hope you're not going to lead us to a cliff edge that eroded down into the surf five years after Dalen stashed the painting there."

But Kevin didn't lead them off into thin air.

Instead, they ended in a bowl-like depression overlooking the ocean, where a couple of stunted trees leaned wildly in the direction of the prevailing winds.

"We're here," Kevin announced.

Everard stepped beside him and stomped a foot down hard. "That's not frozen dirt, folks—it's solid rock. Nothing buried here."

Kevin finally looked away from the GPS, nodding toward the trees. "There's a margin of error up to about twenty feet on these—"

His words were cut off by three gunshots.

19

Spinning around, Liza and her companions scrambled along the rocky terrain toward the sound of the gunfire—heading back the way they'd come. The shots had seemed close—or they could have just seemed unnaturally loud in the windy silence. The only other sound was the remorseless crash of the tide against the base of the cliff.

They arrived at the spot where the two vehicles were parked at the path's end to find Kevin's SUV listing at a strange angle. "The tires!" he yelled in anguish, discovering three of them had gone flat.

Three shots, three tires, Liza realized.

He took a step toward his damaged truck, and then stopped as Mrs. H. came around the bulk of the SUV—closely followed by Howard Frost, who held a small pistol to her head.

"What is going on here?" Liza yelled.

"Have you got it?" Frost said at the same moment.

"You're the one who made the call?" Liza couldn't believe this.

"I'm the one who's got your friend." Howard Frost pushed the muzzle of his gun into the side of Mrs. Halvorsen's head and glared at them. "Now, for the last time, do you have the picture?"

"We think we know where it is," Everard said.

Frost glowered at him. "I figured a cop would come along, no matter what I said. So take out your gun—slowly," he commanded as Ted reached under his jacket. "Just use two fingers." Frost had the muzzle of his pistol almost screwed into Mrs. H.'s ear.

Maybe he's no two-fisted Hollywood private eye, Liza thought, *but he's obviously been in the business long enough to learn the ropes.*

Scowling, Everard daintily drew out his firearm.

"Now toss it under the truck."

The state police investigator followed Frost's order.

"Now, let's get going." Frost frowned as Liza didn't hop to. "Why are you hanging around?"

"We need some digging tools from the SUV," Kevin spoke up.

The insurance investigator pulled Mrs. H. back. "Go get 'em." In moments they were back at the little copse of stunted trees. Kevin started breaking up the cold ground with the mattock. Ted Everard worked with Mrs. H.'s shovel, and Michael had a folding shovel that Kevin kept in his SUV.

They started off well away from any of the tree roots, driving a foot-deep trench across the hard-packed earth. The excavation stretched for a good dozen feet when Michael suddenly stood up from his work. "I think there's something over here!"

Instead of crunching through the soil, the folding shovel had bounced back with a sort of *bonk*! Kevin and Everard came over to concentrate their efforts in the same area. Soon they had uncovered what looked like the sealed end of a six-inch-in-diameter white pipe.

"PVC," Everard said, rapping it with his knuckles.

You'd think we'd be pretty far from anyplace with plumbing out here. Liza forced down her excitement. *This could be it!*

Working together, the men cleared away the soil, revealing a length of pipe about four feet long. Liza noticed that both ends had white plastic caps stuck over them.

"It's a pretty good choice," Everard said. "This stuff is built to form a watertight seal."

"Just get it out and open it," Frost demanded.

Michael and Kevin worked the pipe free, then brought it over to harder ground where Everard waited with the mattock. A couple of carefully judged blows cracked one end near its cap.

"Careful!" Kevin warned as Michael went to pull the jagged crack wider. "That stuff can cut your fingers to the bone."

They used the tip of a shovel to wedge the gap wider until the end finally broke off. Everard reached in carefully to extract a tube of canvas. When he unrolled it, he revealed *Composition in Blue, Red, and Green.*

"The Mondrian," Frost breathed. "The goddam thing that ruined my life—thanks to that bastard Dalen." Mrs. H. gasped, appalled at hearing her brother described that way.

Frost kept the gun at her head. "It's true. I was the top investigator at W.A.G., on the fast track for promotion. They just about promised me a supervisor's job if I recovered the Mondrian."

"But you didn't recover it," Liza said, "and that cost the company millions."

"Millions, plus one supervisory position," Frost's voice went harsh. "Here I am, looking retirement in the face. I could have been—should be—running the department. Instead, I'm still out in the field, trailing some ex-con to find where he hid a painting."

A fanatic's gleam showed in his eyes. "Well, I was going to show those stuffed shirts at the home office, whatever it took. I followed Dalen all over Portland and on to

the Killamook Inn. Then I hid my car by the road and went
back to have a heart-to-heart with him."

"You mean you attacked him, bound him, and tried to
torture him until his heart gave out," Everard said.

"Whatever it took," Frost repeated, his voice back in
that harsh whisper.

"I'd say it was more than was necessary if he died on
you," Michael retorted.

Liza, however, simply stared at the angry old man. "So,
when the sheriff thought he rescued you on the road, you
weren't heading for the inn from your car, you were going
the other way."

Frost nodded. "The weather wasn't so bad when I first
walked to the inn. But by the time I'd hidden Dalen's body
in that cabin, the wind and snow had gone wild. I didn't
think I was going to make it. Then when I saw the cars with
the cherry lights coming, I turned around. You know, my
tracks had already disappeared in the snow."

"So there was no way to tell which way you'd been going. You gave yourself an excellent alibi," Everard reluc-
tantly admitted. "We didn't even consider you as a suspect."

"The doctors said that trip through the deep freeze
nearly killed me," Frost said, "but I thought it was worth it.
Nobody connected me with the murder—except for that
scum Carlowe."

"You knew Rod Carlowe?" Liza asked.

"I knew about him and his methods," Frost replied.
"Never met him before. Maybe, if I'd known what he
looked like . . . but I didn't. Turns out he was following
Dalen, too, recording him on video. He hoped to catch
Dalen in some sort of violation and threaten to get him sent
back to prison."

Frost's jowls wobbled as his face set in a look of dis-
gust. "It was sheer bad luck that Carlowe caught me in his
viewfinder, scouting out the inn shortly after Dalen registered."

"That would destroy your alibi," Michael said.

"It took a while for Carlowe to realize what he had, but then he tried to blackmail me." The old man's voice grated over those words. "He thought I must have gotten something out of Dalen—told me he wanted the inside track."

Frost's grin showed a set of stained teeth. "He didn't know about the gun I'd picked up in a pawn shop years ago. So he was quite surprised when I just shot him as I got in the backseat for his little picture show. Then all I had to do was remove the evidence, and I was home free."

"Except for not having the Mondrian," Liza pointed out.

"But now I do have it," Frost replied. "The Canadian border is just a few hundred miles away. One good thing after all my years in the business—I've got the contacts to turn that painting into a nice little nest egg. And I deserve every penny."

Liza suddenly remembered his bitter speech in Ma's Café, comparing his retirement with Chris Dalen's. For a second, Frost seemed lost in contemplation of that wonderful future of affluence and ease. From the corner of her eye, Liza could see Everard gathering himself for a leap.

But then Frost came back to the here and now, pulling Mrs. H. back and aiming the Saturday night special at the state policeman. "Don't do anything stupid," Frost warned. "Just roll up the painting nice and neat and put it back in the pipe."

"And then?" Everard asked even as he followed Frost's demands.

"Then you can dig that trench a little deeper. I see now that it's still too easy for some would-be hero to try jumping out." He made them all work now. Even Liza had to scoop the dirt out with her bare hands. The exertion left them panting—and standing in a trench nearly three feet deep.

At least we're still breathing, Liza thought as she coughed in the damp, chilly air. *I just hope all this digging doesn't give Frost ideas. How many stories in the* Oregon Daily *talked about the discovery of bodies in shallow graves?* Liza wished her big, fat imagination would just shut up for the time being.

"All right, that's enough," Frost said. "First thing, I want you to throw the pipe with the picture to me."

"I've got a better idea," a voice called out.

Frankie Basso stepped down into the bowl-like depression, a pistol in his hand. "You can throw the picture to me."

20

Liza found herself staring and speechless as Basso gave them all a genial fat-man grin—so out of place coming from behind the big automatic pistol in his hand. He was wearing a sweat suit in fire-engine red and white. It would have made him look like Santa Claus—if Santa went beardless and draped a vicuna camel-hair coat over his outfit.

Basso's eyebrows rose to create wrinkles across his forehead when he spotted Liza. "Well, hello, Ms. Kelly. This is a surprise. And it's great to see you, too, Mr. Shepard."

You'd think this was a class reunion from the way he's beaming at us, Liza thought. *Except for the way he's standing. From there, he can cover all of us, as well as Frost.*

When Basso announced himself, Howard Frost had swung Mrs. Halvorsen around to use her as a human shield—at least a partial shield. Frost wasn't a tall man, but Mr. H. was even shorter. Her head barely came up to the insurance investigator's chest.

At least he didn't have that ugly little pistol poking into his hostage's ear anymore. Now Frost had his gun trained on Fat Frankie's vast bulk.

"I heard you got out of Coastal Correctional yesterday afternoon," Liza said wryly. "For a while, I thought you might be the one who took my friend here." She nodded at Mrs. Halvorsen.

Basso's porky face took on a well-practiced expression of shock. "I can't believe you'd think I would break the law—and on the very day I got out of the joint," he said piously.

Liza shrugged. "What can I say? I was running out of suspects." She glanced over at Frost with his white-knuckled grip on his Saturday night special. "And I didn't even suspect who it turned out to be. Howard Frost, soon to be late of the Western Assurance Group, meet Frank Basso, who has a certain name in organized crime circles."

"Call me Fat Frankie," Basso said in a genial voice. "Everybody else does."

"What do you want?" Frost demanded, his pistol wobbling as badly as his jowls.

"Didn't you hear me the first time? I want the same thing you do—the picture." Liza couldn't help but notice that the semiautomatic in Basso's hand was rock steady.

"So what brings you all the way out here?" Liza asked Basso. *Anything to string this along—to postpone the final showdown,* she thought. *Although I don't know what I'm expecting—the cavalry to come over the hill? The Coast Guard to come steaming up from the horizon? Sheriff Clements dropping down by rope from a passing helicopter?*

None of those happened, but Fat Frankie seemed ready to chat a little more—probably waiting for Howard Frost's quivering arm to fall off.

"Well, it was kind of a spur-of-the-moment thing," he said. "After I left the hospitality of the state, I stopped in to see a business associate who has a house just north of Maiden's Bay."

"I thought people on parole weren't supposed to associate—" Liza began.

Basso gave a hearty chuckle. "Oh, this fellow is no felon. He's a respectable businessman—and it just happens that we have certain business interests in common."

"So what was your business in Maiden's Bay?" Liza wanted to know.

"Actually, it was in Killamook—getting my associate Mr. Tanino sprung from jail," Basso replied. "We were going down to Main Street to talk to a lawyer when we saw a whole convoy of police cars zooming along."

Basso gave Liza his patented avuncular smile—the one that didn't reach his eyes. "I figured it couldn't be a parade in my honor, but I decided to pull into the end of the line. After all, the only big deal on the local law's plate was the Dalen murder—and the missing painting. So I decided to tag along and see if there were any developments I might be able to capitalize on."

He shrugged. "Imagine my surprise when I saw you come out, throw a bunch of digging equipment into an SUV, and then ride off. Well, with a buildup like that, how could I resist? I told my associate to walk the rest of the way to the lawyer's, and I took off after you—at a discreet distance, of course."

"And you carried your law-abiding associate's discreet gun?" Liza couldn't help pointing out.

"Oh, he has this gun quite legally, I'll have you know," Basso said. "As for me carrying it—well, not so legal. That's another reason why I had him stay behind. A solid citizen like him would be too busy worrying over pros and cons instead of taking decisive action. I, however, do not have any such problem."

"So we see," Liza said.

He gave her another of his creepy smiles, then went back to his story. "Holding back the way I had to, I missed that turnoff you took and didn't find out until I got on a long straightaway and didn't spot you up ahead. So I had to backtrack and lost some time. Still, I managed to catch up to you guys in time to hear most of the tale of the painting.

The only bad part was that from where I was standing, I didn't get a look at this famous picture."

Basso nodded to Everard. "Would you mind taking it out of that tube and showing me? You can just spread it on the ground."

That got a strangled sound like a growl from Howard Frost. But he didn't say anything else as Ted Everard did as he was asked.

Like he was going to argue with a guy holding a gun in his hand. Liza had to choke back a bubble of hysterical laughter.

Basso took a quick look at the unfurled Mondrian and shrugged, his expression massively unimpressed. "Is this the three-million-dollar big deal? I got a bathroom that looks like that. Better, even—it's got more colors."

He shrugged again. "Still, three mill is three mill." Basso turned his amiable smile onto Frost. "So, Pops, if you and the old broad will just get in the hole with the others . . ."

Don't do it, Liza silently entreated.

Possibly, just possibly, Frost might have used the trench to keep them all at a physical disadvantage, confiscate their cell phones, and leave them stranded with the disabled SUV. By the time they managed to hoof it out of the park and find some outpost of civilization—Liza couldn't even remember the last town, store, or gas station they'd passed—Dark-horse Howard would be well along on his getaway.

But if Frost got into this damned pit, Liza couldn't imagine Fat Frankie letting any of them leave it alive. Frost, however, didn't move, still holding his position behind Mrs. H. and aiming his little pistol at the gangster.

Fat Frankie's faux joviality slowly dimmed until the mask was completely gone and the face of a professional killer stared out. "Y'know, Grampaw, I wasn't much worried about what you would do with your little lady friend—"

"I'm not his lady friend!" Mrs. H. fumed.

"Whatever. The thing is, you should be worried about *me.* If I pull this trigger, it don't bother me any if I gotta go through her to get to you."

For once, Fat Frankie's face matched his eyes—dead, and deadly.

And, Liza's mind irreverently had to point out, *ungrammatical, too.*

Basso used his free hand to tap the side of the big pistol. "This is the real thing, not some little Saturday night special popgun like you got. You couldn't even get a bullet all the way through Rod Carlowe's skull. My gun can send a bullet through both of you."

Liza gulped, realizing the crime boss wasn't just being brutally frank, he was being frankly brutal. The muzzle of his automatic pointed straight at Mrs. Halvorsen's chest—and at Frost's gut behind it.

"Don't be stupid," Basso warned. "This can go easy—or it can get real messy."

Howard Frost's shoulders slumped as he began bringing his gun hand down. Then he suddenly shoved Mrs. H. to his right as he dived to the left, bringing his pistol up again.

Frankie Basso had the heart of a killer, but he hadn't had much practice lately. His reflexes were a little slow in reacting to Frost's desperate ploy. Both guns went off at the same time, although the boom of Basso's automatic drowned out Frost's shot.

Frost gave a yelp that turned into a high-pitched scream as he flopped to the stony ground. Liza could see a dark, wet discoloration on the right shoulder of his brown polyester parka.

Fat Frankie took one step back, looking down in almost comical surprise at the red stain spreading quickly across the pale, expensive wool on the chest of his overcoat. Then he realized his gun hand had dropped down by his side. Focusing on Frost, he tried to bring his pistol back up—and toppled, inert, just short of the Mondrian he had disparaged.

Okay, maybe Frost's popgun wasn't all that accurate, Liza thought. *But then Fat Frankie was a pretty big target.*

She, Michael, and Kevin had stood frozen in the shallow trench while everything went on. Ted Everard had dropped to one knee. Liza was about to pass a comment on his bravery—or was that common sense? But even as she opened her mouth, Ted burst to his feet with a pistol in his hand. She realized he'd been going for a backup gun in an ankle holster.

In the instant it took Ted to get his gun out, Frost snaked across the mound of earth they had shoveled out, clamped the Mondrian under his injured arm, and aimed his pistol at Everard.

"Get . . . back," the older man gasped as he wobbled, trying to stay upright. "I've shown . . . I'll . . . shoot." His face twisted as he somehow forced himself to move, the unfurled painting held tightly across his chest almost like a shield.

It is *a shield,* Liza realized. *Ted isn't about to risk shooting a hole through a three-million-dollar painting. That's not the way to get off desk duty.*

She could see the struggle between his duty as a cop and prudence on Everard's face as he stood, pistol at the ready, while Frost backed away.

"Why don't you hold it right there," Ted called to him.

"I really don't think so," Frost sneered. "You don't dare shoot at me while I'm holding this." He tried to flap the painting at Everard, went pale, and staggered.

Woops, he figured it out, too, Liza thought.

"Frost, you've got a multimillion-dollar painting and a bleeding bullet wound." Ted's voice was steady. So was his gun. "How far do you think you can get?"

That fanatical gleam came back to the older man's eyes. "I will do anything I need to do, and I will put a bullet into anyone who gets in my way. That will be you if you *don't back off*!" His voice rose to a shout. "After all this, I've got the Mondrian. Nobody can stop me. Nobody!"

Frost was so busy trying to stare Ted down, he didn't realize he was passing Elise Halvorsen's prone figure—until she reached out and grabbed his ankle. She wasn't able to stop him, but she sent him staggering. One of his feet caught Mrs. H. in the side of the head, and she went down again.

Howard Frost reeled off in a new direction, mouthing obscenities as he aimed his gun at the old woman. "Shoot you—"

"Oh my God, stop!" Liza yelled, her eyes going wide with shock as she saw what was about to happen. "You're going to go off the cliff!"

"Shoot you all!" The snarl on Frost's face suddenly changed to an expression of pained astonishment, his face abruptly going gray. His gun hand flew up reflexively to press against his chest. The whole arm jerked, and the pistol discharged. The bullet went harmlessly off into the air. As he lurched back another step, the gun flew from Frost's suddenly nerveless fingers.

Liza began clawing her way out of the excavation. "Stop him!" she screamed at Kevin and Michael. "He's going to fall!"

The Hangover Twins finally stirred to some action. But even as they clambered out of the trench behind Liza, Howard Frost tottered back, both arms clasped against his chest and the painting. His mouth opened to scream, but no sound came out.

Thrusting his pistol into the waistband of his trousers, Ted Everard reached out to Frost.

He was an instant too late.

Frost teetered backward—and disappeared off the cliff.

21

"Guys—the killer—the painting!" Liza knew she was babbling, but even as she dashed forward, a cooler part of her head prevailed.

Frost is gone. Forget him. Mrs. H. is the one who needs help.

Those thoughts made good sense.

Liza veered over toward her prostrate neighbor.

Dropping to her knees, Liza gently stretched a hand to the side of her neighbor's face. "Are you all right?"

"He kicked me on the other side," Mrs. Halvorsen mumbled, her words muffled by dirt.

With Michael and Kevin joining in, they managed to get Mrs. H. on her back and then sitting up. She pressed a hand gingerly against her cheekbone, where a bruise was already developing. "That man was a nasty piece of work," Liza's neighbor declared. "Did I hear him get shot?"

"No, that was when he grabbed his chest and his face went a funny color and then he fell off the cliff." Liza realized the words were tumbling out of her again, and took a long breath to try and calm down.

"Sounds like a heart attack," Mrs. Halvorsen said. "The exact same thing took my husband—except for the falling off the cliff part."

"Liza!" Ted Everard called. She stepped away from Michael and Kevin, who were carefully helping Mrs. H. to her feet.

"I'm all right," Liza heard her neighbor saying as she tried to escape the guys' assistance. "Well, maybe a little shaky."

Liza went to the cliff edge, where Everard was lying prone, looking downward.

"Got a touch of vertigo?" she asked the state cop.

"No, I'm looking at something and don't want to be distracted by footing issues," Ted replied.

Liza dropped to her hands and knees, then lay down and stuck her head over the edge.

She stared down for a long minute, silent.

"Well, finally," Everard said with some satisfaction. "I found something that completely shut up the great Liza Kelly."

"It's just as well you're lying down," she told him. "If you were standing up, I'd probably push you over for making a crack like that."

"And I don't expect I'd be as lucky as our friend Howard here," Ted replied. "How many people go off a hundred-foot cliff, drop a bit more than a yard, and get caught by a bush?"

Liza shuddered as she peered down at the body tangled in the branches of a bush tenaciously clinging to the cliff face. She saw Frost's pale face, those staring eyes . . . "Ted, he's not breathing. Mrs. H. said that it could be something like a heart attack."

"That's what I was thinking," Everard said. "He checked himself out of the hospital against the advice of the doctors after walking through that blizzard. It's possible that he might have developed a blood clot that got shaken loose with all the banging around he went through here."

He went into his pocket. "I'm going to call this in. Hope the cell coverage is decent out here."

"Before you do," Liza told him, "I want you to hold me."

Ted nearly jumped out of his skin at her words. The cell phone almost flew out of the state cop's hands and into the pounding surf below. "Hold you?" he repeated. "You want me to hold you? Now?"

"Yes," Liza replied.

He reached for her shoulders as though to embrace her.

"Not like that. Grab my ankles. I need somebody to anchor me as I go down after that goddam painting. You're the least hung over or strung out person here except for Mrs. H., and she got kicked in the head."

"Yeah?" he muttered, hanging onto her legs as she skooched forward to bend from the waist. "I can't imagine how that happened."

"I can," she said. "Hang on!"

By stretching her arms to the limit, she just managed to catch hold of a corner of the Mondrian. As they pulled the painting to safety, she caught the rest of his words. "Ain't *that* a kick in the head?"

A few days later, Liza walked the few blocks from Hackleberry Avenue down Main Street to the Unitarian Church. The white clapboard structure with the tall steeple looked like something you might find in rural Massachusetts, revealing the New England roots of many of Oregon's early settlers. Liza crossed the street and headed for the church doors. She'd been here for a few weddings and a funeral. The interior was a combination of white paint and heavily varnished pine. It would make a simple and somber background for the last rites for Chris Dalen.

Her heels clicked on the sidewalk as she walked up to the church steps. The day was clear but cold, and the empty street seemed somewhat melancholy.

Well, Liza consoled herself, *at least there's not some jackass shoving a microphone in my face.*

The recovery of the Mondrian had created a brief media frenzy. Downtown Maiden's Bay had been clogged with television vans and camera crews. One more ambitious reporter and her crew got themselves stranded out at Cape Sinestra when their van broke an axle on the way to getting a location shot on the cliff where Howard Frost and Frankie Basso had died. That had been hot news for a day.

Ava Barnes and Michelle Markson, usually adversaries rather than allies, had both been gratified by the amount of coverage. Liza had found her face plastered across newspapers and the airwaves for her role in finding the clue in the sudoku, and her column had gotten plenty of free publicity.

And then Ritz Tarleton, less than a week out of the pokey, had gotten arrested on a DUI charge again. The nation's newsmeisters had weighed the stories in the balance—drunken celebutante versus abstract art. And even though the Mondrian was worth $3 million, the drunken celebrity story was of course the one that the media had led with. The news cycle went on.

I guess that means there'll be a small turnout without the gawkers and idiots, Liza thought as she opened the door.

Inside, the church was packed. No talking heads from television, no true-crime buffs, but all of Elise Halvorsen's friends and neighbors had shown up to support her, even though they didn't know her brother from a hole in the wall.

Liza looked around for a seat. Oh, great. Michael and Kevin were sitting together with a space between them. Michael had brought a suit up with him. He should have brought an overcoat—he looked cold. Liza also recognized the suit Kevin was wearing. The last time she'd seen it had been on their big date before she discovered Dalen's body.

Sheriff Clements was in the last row of pews, a brown wool overcoat over his best khaki uniform. Beside him stood Ted Everard in that loden suit she'd first seen him in.

It looked a lot better with a light gray shirt and a black patterned tie, not to mention being cleaned and pressed.

Jaysol's Dry Cleaners must have been doing banner business for this hoedown, Liza thought.

Up in the front row, Mrs. Halvorsen sat in the purple wool suit she always wore to funerals. She hadn't worn black since she buried her husband. Liza's neighbor was surrounded by a coterie of bemused-looking relatives—her nieces and nephews. Mrs. H. was the last Dalen of her generation.

About halfway down the aisle, Liza spotted a waving hand. Thank heavens, Ava had saved a seat for her. Joining her friend, Liza sat down and listened to some whispered grousing about the lack of national coverage until Pastor Todd came out to lead them in prayer.

Liza knew the pastor to be a good man, but today he showed himself a master preacher as he gave a eulogy that had to be an oratorical nightmare. He'd glossed over Chris Dalen's rotten relationship with his family, how he made his living, where he'd been for the last fifteen years, and how he'd died.

Somehow, Pastor Todd got the job done, remembering Chris as a loving brother who had made some mistakes in life, but who, at the end, had tried to make up for the biggest transgression of his past and managed to assure his sister's future.

Liza glanced over at Ava. *I guess that means the news has gotten out about the reward money.*

The Western Assurance Group had balked at first when Liza applied for the reward—and demanded that it be paid to Elise Halvorsen. When you came right down to it, if it hadn't been for Mrs. H., Liza wouldn't have undertaken to find the painting at all. It had taken some pointed comments from Michelle to one of the senior vice presidents about the value of good publicity versus bad, but the company had finally agreed to pony up for the finder's fee. Taxes would take a healthy bite out of the sum, but Mrs. H.

should end up with enough to live out the rest of her life
comfortably.

Liza rose with the rest of the congregation as the pall-
bearers took the plain wooden coffin from the church. Mrs.
Halvorsen and her relations followed. She was sobbing
quietly, trying to hide it, no doubt unsettled a bit by finding
herself the center of attention.

"Are you going to the cemetery?" Ava asked when they
finally got outside. "You could ride with me."

Recognizing a covert plea for moral support, Liza
agreed. The sermon had exercised a remarkable influence on
Ava, it turned out. Liza's managing editor didn't mention
news or publicity for the entire drive.

The turnout at the graveside was smaller, just the
Halvorsen/Dalen contingent and a few of Mrs. H.'s closer
friends. Liza noticed that the sheriff and Ted Everard also
attended. Pastor Todd kept the ceremonies dignified and
brief, and at last it was over.

When Liza stepped up to offer her condolences, Elise
Halvorsen flung both arms around her in a tight hug. Liza
found her own eyes blurred with tears.

She'd had another nightmare last night—at least it had
started as one. Chris Dalen had erupted spectacularly from
the mattress, pursuing her across the treacherously giving
terrain of the endless bed. But when he'd finally caught up
with her, his eyes had been alive, not staring, and all he'd
done was say, "Thanks."

"Where to now?" Ava asked as they walked away.

"Mrs. H. is having what she calls 'a small collation' at
her house, and I agreed to help with the food," Liza said.

Her friend immediately reverted to managing editor
mode. "And then I hope you'll be getting some work done.
Your cushion frankly needs some padding. You've got a national column now. This is not the time to be goofing off."

"Then let's hope nobody else I know gets murdered
anytime soon," Liza said.

That shut Ava up.

As the crowd began to disperse, Liza spotted two more familiar figures—Michael and Kevin.

Then she realized they were both bearing down on her.

She hadn't exactly been avoiding them. In fact, it had been more the other way around. Kevin and Michael had been a long time getting over their humiliating defeat in the drinking contest at the Famished Farmer and their less than stellar performance the morning after.

Judging from the way they were almost elbowing one another to get to her first, Liza figured their egos were definitely on the mend.

Michael arrived, fractionally in the lead. "Hey, Liza."

Now that he was here, he seemed to lose confidence. Kevin spoke up. "Valentine's Day is coming up, and we want to know—well, I want to know if you and I—"

"Or you and I," Michael put in.

"Oh, Valentine's Day," Liza said. "You know, guys, that's turned into a pretty adult holiday lately."

They nodded, their tongues all but hanging out.

"So I decided to go with the one adult involved in this last adventure."

By luck, Ted Everard passed by at just that moment. Liza hooked his arm.

"That's why Ted and I are going to Portland for that weekend."

They walked off, arm in arm, with what felt like half of Maiden's Bay staring after them, openmouthed in shock.

Even by Michelle's high standards, it was a perfect exit.

Liza smiled.

Sudo-cues

Through the Looking Glass

Written by Oregon's own leading sudoku columnist, Liza K

How often do you find yourself working through the middle of a sudoku and saying nasty things about the person who created the puzzle? I'm guilty of that, and I make a living out of devising the darned things.

However, while recently conducting a class for beginning solvers, I gave them a chance to find out how the other side lives for their final project. I thought I'd kept it simple, giving each participant a solution and the job of removing matching pairs of clues to create a symmetrical, thirty-clue sudoku.

A friend who also took the challenge gave this report. "I did what you asked, checked the final product, and found that I had a puzzle with two possible solutions. When I switched around a couple of other pairs of clues, I wound up with twelve possible solutions. My next fix brought the possible solutions up past a hundred."

The class didn't do so well, either.

Which leads, indirectly, to this article, where I'll attempt to show the method I use to create a very simple puzzle. Don't look for X-Wings or similar esoterica. This will be a puzzle solvable by the simplest techniques.

The first step is to create a gridwork with a symmetrical design. Here, gray spaces represent the final sudoku—they'll become clues. The white spaces we'll call blanks—they'll be blank in the finished puzzle.

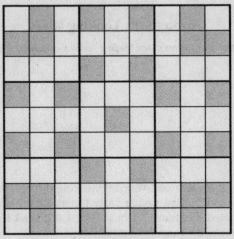

STEP 1

You can choose any of the magic digits 1 through 9 to start. I'll start at the end of the line, setting up a classic Hidden Single situation. This technique works on the basic sudoku rule that a number can appear only once in a box, one of the nine-space subgrids in a puzzle. So, if a particular number is present in the boxes on either side of a given box (or above and below it), that means there are only three spaces in the third box where that number can be found. With clues or filled-in spaces, the number of available spaces can be even smaller. In fact, there may be only one space.

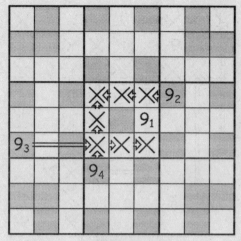

STEP 2

In Step 2, 9_1 shows the only space available in the center box. The placement of 9_2, 9_3, and 9_4 in clue spaces prohibits the placement of 9s in the other rows and columns for the box. We don't need to worry about the empty gray space. In the final puzzle, that will be occupied by other clues.

So, we've placed the first four of the nine 9s for this puzzle. Can we place others? We'll aim to fix digits in blank spaces.

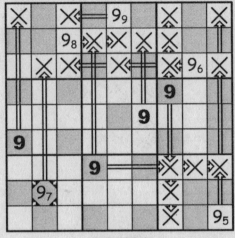

STEP 3

Looking at the lower right box in Step 3, we see that the already placed clues 9_2 and 9_4 prohibit the placement of 9s in most of the box. With three additional spaces taken up by clues, there's only one space available, which we've filled with 9_5.

Next, we move to the box in the upper right. The newly placed 9_5 prohibits placements of 9s in the open spaces in one column. Placed clue 9_2 prohibits 9s in another column. Since we're trying to avoid placing digits in clue spaces, this leaves one blank, which we'll fill with 9_6.

Another technique for fixing numbers in place is to use a clue space to set up placements. Setting up clue 9_7 in the lower left-hand box prohibits any other 9s there. It also affects the upper left-hand box, helping to reduce the number of legal squares to two. Placing 9_8 in one of those inevitably fixes the position of 9_9 in the top center box, and vice versa.

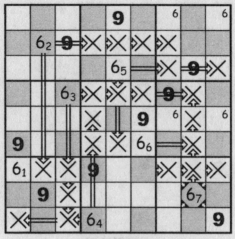

STEP 4

We've picked 6 as the new number to go with in Step 4. Looking at the lower left-hand box, we've created a hidden single for 6_1 using clues 6_2, 6_3, and 6_4. Now look at the top center box. Clues take up four of the available spaces. The already placed 9 takes up a fifth space, and the placement of clue 6_2 prohibits 6s in the central row. This leaves only one available empty space, where we'll place 6_5. The central box in the puzzle has only one clue space and one space occupied with a 9. But the placement of clues around the box prohibit 6s in all but one space, where we've placed 6_6.

Placing 6_7 as shown in the lower right-hand box prohibits 6s in the center column of the right-hand stack of boxes, but leaves some uncertainty in placing a 6 in either of the remaining columns. Let's mark the possible locations for the time being and move on.

STEP 5

As more clues appear in the puzzle grid, we may be able to set up placements with fewer clues. Because of the existing 9s and the arrangement of clue spaces, we only need two clues to establish 7_1 as a hidden single in the lower right-hand box.

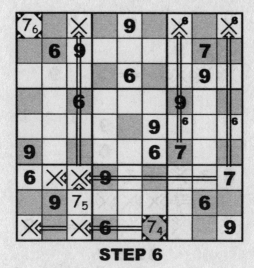

STEP 6

We'll start off Step 6 by placing 7_4 in the bottom center box. Between the squares that this newly placed clue prohibits, and the squares prohibited by already placed clue 7_1, there's only one open space in the lower left-hand box available to place 7_5.

Now take a look at Row 1 at the top of the puzzle. As the long arrows and "prohibited" signs show, 7s that have already been placed account for every open space in the row except for the very first one—and that's where we'll place 7_6.

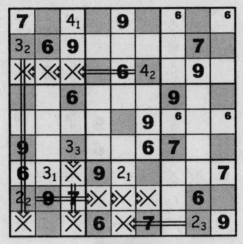

STEP 7

With Step 7, we'll try to establish some other numbers on the grid. Working down the left-hand stack of boxes, we can set up a hidden single situation for 3_1 in the lower left-hand box by placing clues 3_2 and 3_3 as shown.

Then, running across the lowermost tier of boxes, placing clues 2_2 and 2_3 as shown prohibits all but one open space for 2_1 in the bottom center box.

When we look at the upper left-hand corner box, we see that clue spaces and filled-in spaces allow us to use only one clue at 4_2 to place 4_1 at the top of the third column.

STEP 8

Let's see how much farther we can take things by placing 2s. If we establish 2_4 in the clue space in the right-center box, we can place 2_5 in a legal space in the left-center box. The grid is beginning to get crowded now, so this may be the last of that sort of placement.

Putting 2_6 in the upper middle box pretty much forces the placement of 2_7—that's the only legal space in the upper right-hand box, since the only empty spaces in the left top box are in the third row. And looking at that upper-left box, we see that existing clues prohibit 2s in all but one space on that row, so we can place 2_8.

Next, let's look at Row Six. Existing clues prohibit the placement of 2s in every blank space but one, so that fixes the place for 2_9. Now we've placed all the 9s and all the 2s.

Let's look at the top middle box and see if we can start placing 1s. Filled-in spaces and clues leave only the middle row clear. We can easily set 1_1 in place with clues at 1_2 and 1_3.

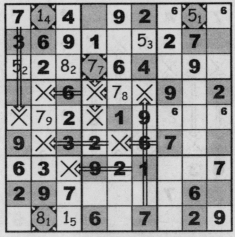

STEP 9

In Step 9, we'll start off trying to place some more 1s. Establishing 1_4 in the clue space in the upper left-hand box, we can fix 1_5 in the lower left box. While there are two open spaces in the third column in the box, an existing clue prohibits the placement of 1s except where shown.

Moving in reverse now, the placement of 8_1 in the center column of the lower left box forces 8_2 in the upper left—that's the only legal space where we can put an eight.

Let's start off the 5s by placing 5_1 on the clue space in the upper right-hand box. Finding 5_2 is pretty obvious—it's the only empty space in the upper-left box. And let's place 5_3 on a legal space in the top-center box before it gets too crowded.

Placing 7_7 in the clue space in the top-center box prohibits 7s in two blank spaces in the central box. Already placed clues eliminate two spaces more. Only one legal space remains, and that's where we've put 7_8. This leaves the left-center box as the only one without a 7. Existing clues (including the just placed 7_8) eliminate all the open spaces in the box except for one. Placing 7_9 there lets us complete another set of numbers.

7	1	4		9	2	6	5	6
3	6	9	1		5	2	7	4_3
5	2	8	7	6	4		9	
1_6		6		7		9	4_4	2
8_5	7	2		1	9	6		6
9		3	2		6	7	1_7	8_3
6	3	5_4	9	2	1		8_4	7
2	9	7					6	
4_5	8	1	6		7		2	9

STEP 10

In Step 10, we'll need to fix a couple more clues to proceed. Setting 8_3 in the right-bottom box fixes 8_4 in the box below—that's the only legal space left in Column Eight. We can also place an 8 in the left-center box. The rightmost column in the box is completely filled, and an existing 8 in the box below eliminates the empty spaces in the center column. That leaves one remaining empty space, where we put 8_5. In that same box, placing 1_6 in a clue space, along with the existing clue in the central box, fixes 1_7 in the center-right subgrid.

Let's look at the situation for 4s. We'd placed only two up to now, in the top-left and top-center boxes. However, since we've placed some other clues in the top-right box, there's only one legal space free to take a 4, so 4_3 goes in the clue space as shown.

There are only two available legal spaces for 4s in the Column Eight so let's fix one with 4_4. And there's only one space left in Column One, and that takes 4_5.

7	1	4		9	2	8_7	5	6_7
3	6	9	1	8_6	5	2	7	4
5	2	8	7	6	4		9	
1	5_6	6		7		9	4	2
8	7	2		1	9	6_8		
9	4_6	3	2	5_5	6	7	1	8
6	3	5	9	2	1	4_7	8	7
2	9	7					6	
4	8	1	6		7		2	9

STEP 11

To start off Step 11, let's look at the intersection of Column Two and Row Six. If we were to start looking for candidates, we'd find that the space can only take a 4 or a 5. So can the other remaining space. However, that space intersects a 4 in the right-middle box. That means we can place 5_6 and 4_6 as shown, as well as 5_5.

In Row Two, there's only one space left, which takes 8_6. An existing 8 in the top left box, plus clues in the middle-right and bottom-right boxes zero in on one possible space for an 8 in the upper-right box. That's where we've placed 8_7. That space, by the way, is one of the four "possible" spaces for 6s. An 8 in that space means a 6 in the space at the end of the line, shown as 6_7. It also places a 6 two spaces to the left and four spaces down, 6_8.

Row Seven has one space left, which is filled by 4_7.

7	1	4	3_4	9	2	8	5	6
3	6	9	1	8	5	2	7	4
5	2	8	7	6	4		9	
1	5	6	8_8	7	3_5	9	4	2
8	7	2	4_8	1	9	6	3_6	5_8
9	4	3	2	5	6	7	1	8
6	3	5	9	2	1	4	8	7
2	9	7	5_7		8_9		6	
4	8	1	6		7		2	9

STEP 12

For the next step, let's start by looking at Row One, where a single remaining empty space takes 3_4. Column Four has three spaces left, which could take an 8, a 5, or a 4. Row Four, the topmost row with a blank in Column Four, already includes a 5 and a 4. That places 8_8. A 5 placed in the same box (one space to the right, two spaces down) eliminates all candidates but 4_8, placed as shown. That leaves 5_7 in the bottom blank in the column.

Row Four now has a single blank space, which is filled by 3_5. Intersecting that space, Column Six now has only one blank, which is filled with 8_9.

Column Eight also has a single open space, leaving 3_6 to fill it. That leads to a chain interaction with Row Five, where the last open space takes 5_8.

We're almost down to the end now, so we have to take care.

7	1	4	3	9	2	8	5	6
3	6	9	1	8	5	2	7	4
5	2	8	7	6	4	1_9	9	3_8
1	5	6	8	7	3	9	4	2
8	7	2	4	1	9	6	3	5
9	4	3	2	5	6	7	1	8
6	3	5	9	2	1	4	8	7
2	9	7	5	4_9	8	3_9	6	1_8
4	8	1	6	3_7	7	5_9	2	9

STEP 13

Starting off lucky Step 13, let's look at Row Nine, specifically, the intersection with Column Seven. Checking the bottom left and bottom center boxes, we find two 5s already placed. That forces the blank space to become 5_9. Similarly, in Row Eight, Column Five, existing 4s force the placement of 4_9. The blank space below, the last in Column Five, therefore becomes 3_7.

This leaves four spaces creating a sort of rectangle between Columns Seven and Nine and Rows Three and Eight, which can take either a 3 or a 1. If these last digits could be interchangeably placed, all our work goes for nothing—you don't have a sudoku unless you have one unique solution.

Luckily, we have a single clue space left. That means we can force the placement of the remaining digits.

Putting 1_8 in the clue space fixes 3_8 five spaces above. Then 1_9 becomes the last space filled in Row Three, and 3_9 completes the puzzle in Row Eight.

We did it! Here's what the puzzle looks like with just the clues:

	1		3		2		5	
3	6						7	4
		7		4				
1		6				9		2
				1				
9		3				7		8
			9		1			
2	9						6	1
	8		6		7		2	

FINISHED PUZZLE

Try it and see whether your solution matches the chain of logic that went into developing the sudoku. Remember, though, if you want a hint, look in front of the puzzle—not in back!

And if you decide to try and create some more sudoku, just bear in mind—you may end up swearing just as much during the creating as you do in the solving.

However you decide to go, remember to have some fun along the way.

Puzzle Solutions

Puzzle from page 12

8	2	6	3	4	9	7	1	5
9	4	5	6	7	1	8	3	2
3	7	1	5	2	8	6	9	4
1	9	8	7	5	4	3	2	6
4	6	7	2	9	3	5	8	1
2	5	3	1	8	6	4	7	9
7	3	9	4	1	5	2	6	8
5	1	2	8	6	7	9	4	3
6	8	4	9	3	2	1	5	7

Puzzle from page 90

5	3	6	9	1	4	2	8	7
2	7	8	5	3	6	9	1	4
9	4	1	2	7	8	3	5	6
4	1	9	3	6	7	8	2	5
7	8	5	1	4	2	6	9	3
6	2	3	8	5	9	7	4	1
1	5	2	7	9	3	4	6	8
3	9	4	6	8	1	5	7	2
8	6	7	4	2	5	1	3	9

Puzzle from page 120

5	8	3	2	7	1	4	6	9
6	7	4	8	3	9	5	1	2
1	2	9	4	5	6	7	3	8
7	9	8	1	4	3	2	5	6
4	3	1	6	2	5	8	9	7
2	5	6	9	8	7	1	4	3
8	1	7	3	9	4	6	2	5
9	4	2	5	6	8	3	7	1
3	6	5	7	1	2	9	8	4

Puzzle from page 213

7	1	4	3	9	2	8	5	6
3	6	9	1	8	5	2	7	4
5	2	8	7	6	4	1	9	3
1	5	6	8	7	3	9	4	2
8	7	2	4	1	9	6	3	5
9	4	3	2	5	6	7	1	8
6	3	5	9	2	1	4	8	7
2	9	7	5	4	8	3	6	1
4	8	1	6	3	7	4	2	9